WHEN STARS RISE AT MIDNIGHT

MIDNIGHT STARS SAGA

BOOK TWO

TESS THOMPSON

WHEN STARS RISE AT MIDNIGHT

1

ESTELLE

I was to be Mrs. Wainwright. My latest false name. I was no longer Estelle Sullivan, my God-given name, or the second name I'd assumed, Stella McCord. Now, I would be Mrs. Estelle Wainwright. If I were to continue this way, I'd have a dozen of them before I went to meet my maker.

My new role as Mrs. Wainwright, a pious, respectable widow living alone in New York City, could not be further from the truth. In reality, I was an unmarried woman who had given birth to an illegitimate daughter. I'd been forced to give my infant to my twin sister and her husband, who would raise her as their own. As Mrs. Wainwright, I was to live in the apartment provided by my benefactor, Percival Bancroft.

One tiny detail? I happened to have fallen in love with Percival. A married man. One who remained faithful to his mentally ill wife, even though she was under close watch and care at an asylum for the insane, instead of by his side, helping to raise their daughter.

However, I could not allow the facts to take away from the relief that came from a warm place to stay and a full belly. The months since I'd been on my own, I'd not been at all certain I would not die alone on the streets of this dangerous city.

Therefore, I found myself on the evening of Christmas in the year 1922 in an opulent apartment in Upper Manhattan, with my new name and only Penelope, my maid from the time I was staying with the Bancrofts, as a familiar face. She had been sent over to care for me, as well as a cook, both provided by the Bancrofts. For all intents and purposes, I was a kept woman. Or, at least, that's what it would look like to anyone who didn't understand the honorable nature of Percival Bancroft. In exchange for his generosity, he expected only friendship and the pleasure of my company for dinner on Saturday evenings.

At the sound of rapping on the front door, I hurried across the room to the foyer, expecting to welcome Mrs. Landry, my new cook, of whom I knew nothing other than that she'd been trained by Mrs. Bancroft's cook and that her husband had perished in the Great War.

I don't know what I'd expected, but it was not the young woman in front of me now. Older than I by about ten years, if I were to guess, she possessed a head of thick hair the glossy color of which evoked images of the butterscotch candies I'd so delighted over as a youngster, broad cheekbones, light green eyes, and a small mouth. She carried a basket slung over one arm.

"You must be Mrs. Landry?" I asked.

"Yes ma'am."

"I'm Mrs. Wainwright," I said, the name so foreign in my mouth. "Welcome and Merry Christmas."

"Thank you, I'm pleased to be here," Mrs. Landry said.

Penelope's brown eyes shone from her round face as she greeted her. "I'm Penelope, the miss's maid."

Mrs. Landry bobbed her head. "Pleased to make your acquaintance. My apologies for not being here to welcome you earlier. I wanted to get to the market before they closed, but I had no luck. I'm afraid you'll have to dine on bread and cheese tonight. I'm terribly sorry."

"It's no trouble at all," I said. "Considering how little I've had to eat over the last few weeks, any food at all is welcome. Anyway, you didn't have much notice of my arrival. Dr. Bancroft has left a bottle of champagne on ice." I gestured toward the bar cabinet. "Between that, bread, and cheese, I'd say we're having a feast. Shall we pop the cork and enjoy a Christmas toast?"

"Champagne? With us?" Mrs. Landry asked, sounding scandalized. "I haven't seen a bottle of champagne in quite some time."

"Even during Prohibition, somehow people find it in their cellars. Regardless, it's Christmas, and I'm all alone in a new place, as are you two. We should enjoy a glass by the fire, don't you agree? Unless you'd rather not?"

"No, I'd love to. It's unexpected, that's all." Mrs. Landry's mouth lifted into a shy smile. "I'll be right back to open the bottle."

"Please, allow me," Penelope said. "While you put everything away in the kitchen."

"Thank you. I shan't be long." Mrs. Landry shrugged out of her coat, slung it over her other arm, and headed toward the kitchen, leaving me with Penelope.

"Mrs. Wainwright. That'll take some getting used to, miss," Penelope whispered.

"For me too," I said. "Regardless, I'm pleased to see you. I wasn't sure I'd lay eyes upon you again."

"I was devastated when they told me they'd sent you away."

"Is that what they said? Sent me away?" Although it was the truth, it bothered me to hear it described thus.

"No, they didn't tell us anything other than you'd left. However, a few of the staff overheard the goings-on and reported it back to the rest of us."

Nothing went unnoticed by the servants. This had not been unknown to me previously. I'd been raised in a house with dozens of staff. My twin sister and I had been aware of the ways they'd gossiped about my family and others.

"It was that brother, wasn't it?" Penelope asked. "Simon Price? Was he the one who made them send you away?"

"I'm afraid so," I said. Simon was Perceval's brother-in-law. When he'd discovered who I really was, he'd told the Bancrofts, and they'd been forced to ask me to leave. I could not blame them, given the nature of the complicated web between our two families. Had I known that the day I met Percival on the train, I would not have allowed myself to follow him home or be nursed back to health by his mother.

I wouldn't think of any of that now. A roaring fire in the hearth warmed the room. We had champagne and a lovely, if simple, supper to enjoy. Just yesterday, I'd been contemplating going to work in a brothel. Safety and warmth were welcome gifts despite the complex reasons behind them.

Penelope popped the cork from the champagne bottle. Soon, she'd poured three glasses and had them arranged neatly on the coffee table by the fire. Mrs. Landry returned with a tray carrying a fresh loaf of bread, a chunk of creamy cheese, and slices of ham.

"Please sit," I said. "For tonight, we'll not worry about protocol. I'd be appreciative of the company."

They obeyed as if I were the lady of the house, which I suppose I was—a far cry from the life of destitution I'd faced only days before.

"First, a toast. To having a warm place to sleep and full stomachs," I said, raising my glass.

We clinked glasses and took sips of the bubbly wine that tickled my nose.

Soon, we'd devoured most of the food. Apparently, I wasn't

the only hungry one. It made me wonder. What kinds of lives did they have before Percival hired them?

"I'd like to be up-front about something," I said. "Unfortunately, I'm going to have to pretend to be someone I'm not. But I'd rather not do that in my own home. Doctor Bancroft has assured me you're discreet, Mrs. Landry?"

"Yes, ma'am." Mrs. Landry's high cheekbones flushed pink. "At my last position, the housekeeper insisted on discretion. She allowed no gossip in or out of the house. Regardless, I have no one to tell. As you may know, my husband was killed in the war. I have no children. My mother and father passed away years ago."

"I'm sorry about your husband," I said.

"Thank you. It's been a difficult several years," Mrs. Landry said. "A few months back, I was dismissed."

"May I ask why?" I asked. "Whatever you say, I promise not to think poorly of you."

Pink dotted her cheeks as she lowered her gaze. "I'd rather not say."

"You can say whatever it is," Penelope said. "Miss Stella won't think any worse of you. She's not that way."

"No, I most certainly will not. I have a sordid tale of my own."

Mrs. Landry sighed and looked as if she were about to burst into tears. "The master of the house expected certain things I did not wish to give him."

"Oh, yes, I see," I said with a sigh. "I'm sorry. I can safely say I will not expect anything of the sort."

Penelope giggled, which caused me to follow suit. A second later, Mrs. Landry did the same.

"Doctor Bancroft has told the landlord and other tenants that I am Stella Wainwright. I'm afraid I'll have to ask you to be part of my lie. Mrs. Wainwright is a wealthy widow with no children. This is the only way I could seem respectable."

5

"Societal rules that have no base in truth," Mrs. Landry said rather hotly.

"I do agree," I said, smiling.

"How did your pretend husband die?" Penelope asked, reaching for a piece of cheese.

"Goodness me, we didn't decide that," I said sheepishly. "Dr. Bancroft and I only came up with the story this morning. It's not well-plotted, as you can see."

"Spanish flu?" Mrs. Landry suggested.

"Excellent idea," I said. "Poor Mr. Wainwright. He was such a good man."

More giggling.

"What are we to say about where you come from? Your family and all that?" Mrs. Landry asked, leaning forward expectedly, clearly interested in the game of it all. This gave me some relief, as I was worried it would hurt her to hear of a dead husband who never existed when she had a very real one who had.

"It's vague," I said. "I'm from a wealthy family no one's heard of, which is preferable to the one I had."

"Had?" Mrs. Landry asked.

"Let's have some more champagne," I said, reaching for the bottle.

"No, miss, you must allow me to pour," Penelope said. "Please, I have to earn my keep."

"By all means," I said, pulling my hand from the bottle.

"Since you were up-front with me, I shall do the same," I said. "My story's rather long and sad, but here it is," I told them about my dead fiancé, who had left me with child. "Because of this, I had no choice but to give my infant daughter to my twin sister and to start a new life here in the city." I left out the part about my father being a gangster. That could wait for another time. I didn't want to scare either of them away.

"What about your family? Did they discard you?" Mrs. Landry asked.

"Yes, I'm not welcome to return. I was left with nothing and forced to start a new life here in the city. Having just given birth, I got on the train heading here. Fortunately, kind Dr. Bancroft offered to help me, taking me home with him. Mrs. Bancroft nursed me back to health. When I was well enough, I began to assist Mrs. Bancroft in her volunteer work looking after the poor and infirm in some of the poorest neighborhoods in the city."

"I, too, lost a baby," Mrs. Landry said quietly. "Stillbirth. John, my husband, was already overseas by then. I've no family, leaving me alone to grieve."

"I'm sorry," I said. "That's horrific. And very sad."

Mrs. Landry used a napkin to dab at the corners of her eyes. "Yes, it was. The last few years have been hard."

"You're here now," I said.

"By the grace of God," Mrs. Landry said. "Why are you no longer staying with the Bancrofts?"

"For reasons I cannot go into now, the Bancrofts had to ask me to leave. I spent months trying to find work but had no luck. Finally, I was forced to consider working in a brothel."

"No, miss." Penelope gasped, and her hand flew to her mouth.

"Yes. That's where Doctor Bancroft found me." I grew warm, remembering his reaction when he'd found me there. He'd been angry and appalled, both of which led him to offer me this place to live. "He offered this apartment so that I wouldn't have to do such a terrible thing to keep from starving."

Mrs. Landry and Penelope exchanged a glance.

"It's not what you think," I said. "Dr. Bancroft takes his marriage vows as sacred. He's asked only for friendship in exchange for taking care of me, for which I'm grateful."

"I've never heard of such a thing before now," Penelope

mumbled under her breath. "Men are not usually so benevolent."

"He's a remarkable man," I said.

Falling in love with another woman's husband was never what I'd imagined for myself when I was a little girl. No one would wish to be tortured in such a way. Pining for a man married to another was an endless ache, a combination of guilt, self-hatred, and longing that threatened to smother me each and every day. Regardless, Percival and I had agreed that we could not act on our feelings. To do so would hurt too many people. Worse, it would be a betrayal of his marriage vows, taken before God. Neither of us could be that selfish, even though I wished more than anything he could be by my side.

I'd not thought it possible to fall in love again after I lost Constantine. However, during the months I spent in the Bancroft house, I came to understand that the human heart had a remarkable capacity for love, even after such a tremendous loss.

"What about you, Penelope?" Mrs. Landry asked. "How did you find yourself here?"

"I have a big, rambunctious family, but they live far away. I send them money whenever I can. With seven children, not including me, now that I'm on my own. It has not been easy for my father to provide for us."

"What is it that he does for a living?" Mrs. Landry asked.

"We have a small farm in upstate New York. Some years have been better than others. Now that I can send part of my salary home, it's been easier for them."

"You must miss them," I said softly.

"I do." Penelope gazed into her glass. "But I cannot dwell on my lonesomeness, only my blessings." She went on to explain to Mrs. Landry that she had been hired by the Bancrofts and had been delighted when they asked if she would like to work for me and live here at the apartment.

"I've never worked for only one member of a household," Mrs. Landry said. "I'm more accustomed to a full kitchen."

"I hope you won't be bored," I said.

"No, ma'am, I'm sure I won't be."

We were interrupted by a knock on the front door. "Who could that be?" I asked out loud. "No one knows I'm here."

Both my companions shot up as if suddenly pushed from behind.

Penelope smoothed her dress. "I'll answer. I hope whomever it is does not smell the champagne on my breath." Her eyes widened. "What if it's a cop?"

"I doubt that," I said. "But we'll hide the hooch if we need to." I must have been slightly tipsy, as I suddenly found myself very amusing.

Penelope hustled to the front door and opened it, with me following closely behind. A young man stood there, dressed in a shabby suit. Still, it was finely cut and made of good material, hinting at better times.

"May I help you, sir?" Penelope asked.

"I reside across the hallway. I come to welcome you to the building and wish you all a Merry Christmas."

I gestured for him to step inside from the cold, drafty hallway. "Do come in. I'm...Mrs. Wainwright."

"It's a pleasure to meet you." The man held out his hand. "I'm Joseph Foster. Welcome to the building."

I took a good look at him. Slight and of medium height, he appeared to be in his mid-thirties, with wavy light brown hair and gray eyes behind wire-rimmed glasses. His worn shoes had been polished, but it was obvious they were as old as his suit. How did he afford to live in this building? This was one of the finest in the city, with views of the river.

"Thank you. Would you care for some champagne and something to eat?" I asked. "We're enjoying bread and cheese."

He swallowed and seemed on the verge of declining, but I insisted. The hunger in his eyes was unmistakable.

I introduced him to Mrs. Landry, who stood near the fire, looking uneasy.

"Since it's Christmas, we're all sitting down together," I said to Mr. Foster. Hopefully, he would not think this strange. To his credit, if he did, it certainly didn't show in his face. "Please do sit."

Penelope had already gone to the cabinet for another glass.

Meanwhile, Mrs. Landry had started to inch toward the kitchen. I stopped her, calling out to come back and enjoy the rest of her champagne.

Looking as if I'd required her to walk toward the gallows, she did as I asked.

When we were all settled, and Mr. Foster had a plate piled with bread and cheese, I asked how long he'd lived in the building.

"All my life. My grandfather owned the apartment for decades. He left it to my father. My father left it to me. It's all I have left if you want to know the truth."

"And what is it you do for a living, Mr. Foster?" I asked.

"Please, call me Joseph."

"Joseph, please share with us what you do," I said again.

"I'm a reporter for *The New York Times*. The obituary section." This last part was said with a noted degree of humility. In fact, he seemed embarrassed.

That explained his meager attire. Obituary writers were known to make less than other reporters, who frankly didn't make much either.

"I'm also working on a novel." Joseph pushed his spectacles further up his nose. He was nice-looking, I decided, if not particularly striking. There was a sensitivity in his eyes that I fancied mirrored his soul. It did not surprise me in the least that he'd chosen writing as a profession, as he seemed the type to possess keen observational skills. I'd never thought about writing myself, but knew from my love of reading that authors had a fine sense of detail.

"How is the novel coming along?" I asked.

"Slow," he said. "One sentence at a time. If you hear the click-clack of a typewriter, that's me."

"What kind of story? Is it a mystery?" Penelope asked, eyes shining and cheeks flushed from the champagne. "I love mysteries. Have you read *The Mysterious Affair at Styles?*"

Joseph nodded, seemingly pleased by her enthusiasm. "I have indeed, but I'm not writing a mystery. Rather, it's a family saga about a man who loses his fortune through a series of bad decisions. I admit this with utter mortification, but it's based on my own family. My father, mostly."

Penelope's brow wrinkled as if she had not understood a word he said. Mrs. Landry, on the other hand, had not taken her eyes off him.

"It sounds fascinating," Mrs. Landry said, smiling. "Are any of your characters the family cook?"

I chuckled, amused by the color in her cheeks, which matched Penelope's quite well. The champagne had gone to our heads. I'd not felt this good in ages.

"No, I cannot say I have the cook's point of view in the book," Joseph said. "But perhaps I should revisit that idea?"

"If you need any information about what it's really like to cook for a wealthy family, do let me know," Mrs. Landry said.

"I will indeed." They smiled at each other for a few seconds, seeming to have forgotten the existence of myself and Penelope. Smitten? How wonderful it would be if they were to fall in love right under my nose. Someone should be happy. If not me, then perhaps Mrs. Landry.

I was struck with an idea. "We should have a book society."

"What, may I ask, is a book society?" Penelope smiled, her dimples making small indentations on both sides of her mouth.

There was a quality about Penelope, with her white-blond hair and wide-set eyes, that reminded me of a small fairy that might live in a tree. As children, my sister and I had enjoyed many hours of play in our secret garden, where we imagined fairies living in the hollows of trees.

"It's a meeting of sorts," I said. "Where friends all agree to read the same book and discuss it over tea or sherry." I wasn't entirely sure if this was a common practice, but it seemed like a wonderful idea. Determined to make a life for myself comprising more than hours and hours isolated in my apartment, I had to be creative. For such a long time it had felt as if my life were over, but Percival had given me a new one.

"This sounds like a splendid idea," Joseph said.

"I'd enjoy being included too," Mrs. Landry said.

"What about Mr. Landry?" Joseph asked. "Does he enjoy reading?"

"I'm afraid he's passed away." Mrs. Landry glanced toward the fire. "In the war."

"My sincere condolences," Joseph said. "And you, Mrs. Wainwright? Do you have a Mr. Wainwright hidden somewhere?" I knew from the way he asked the question with just a slight edge —like one might expect from a detective—that he'd seen Percival and me arrive earlier.

"My husband died of the Spanish flu." I did not have to pretend to grieve, simply replacing the loss of my daughter and family for the pretend husband.

"Again, my condolences." Joseph tugged at his left ear. "May I ask who escorted you in this afternoon?"

"That is…my godfather." Where had that come from? He was much too young to be my godfather unless he'd been granted that role when he was ten years old. I suppose that was possible. Oh, these tangled webs I wove were already starting to unravel. "He promised my family he'd look out for me. They're dead too." I blurted that last part out. Acting, clearly, was not one of my gifts.

"And you, Mr. Foster?" Penelope asked, saving me from saying anything further. "Do you have any family left?"

"No. My mother died when I was young, and my father about ten years ago. He was fond of drink."

"That settles it, then," I said. "We shall be a society of lonesome book lovers."

"I have a few friends who might like to join us," Joseph said. "If that is all right?"

"Yes, of course." I pushed the tray closer to him. "Please, eat. It's Christmas."

"Shall I open more champagne, miss?" Penelope asked. "Dr. Bancroft left several more bottles."

"Why not? We must eat and drink and be merry."

For the next fifteen minutes, we chatted about less serious things than our misfortunes. Joseph told us a little about his work at the newspaper. Penelope coaxed into a relaxed state, shared more about her family and the hilarious antics of her five brothers and two sisters.

By nine, the bread and cheese were gone, and Mrs. Landry insisted we allow her to make us each an omelet. The next thing I knew, we were all in the kitchen. The three of us gathered around the small wooden table on the other side of the butcher's block while Mrs. Landry got out butter and eggs and heated up a frying pan. We all watched as she effortlessly whipped together the eggs with the rapid movement of a fork and then poured it into the pan of melted butter. She lifted the pan from the heat, tossing the eggs about, and then carefully folded them before slipping another spoonful of butter over the top.

"Where did you learn to do such sorcery?" Joseph asked.

Mrs. Landry tugged on the front of her apron, blushing with embarrassment. She was not accustomed to attention, that much was clear. "I trained under a remarkable cook. She studied in France, where she learned the fine art of sauces and other complicated dishes."

"The French know how to make everything beautiful," Joseph said. "And now it appears you do as well."

Since Joseph was our guest, we insisted that he have the first one. Upon the first bite, he closed his eyes and moaned. "It's magnificent."

Soon, to our delight, we were all digging into our omelets. Penelope and I had to agree that they were divine.

"To think, two days ago, I was so hungry I was about to chew my arm off," I said. "Now I'm eating like a French duchess."

"Where were you two days ago?" Joseph asked.

"It's a rather long story that I'll tell you about some other time." I must deflect until I came up with a story that I could remember. "Suffice it to say, my fortune has changed, thanks to my kind...godfather."

An understanding flashed in Joseph's eyes. I knew what he thought. However, I couldn't say anything that would change his mind, so I left it alone. Anyway, we were having such fun. In addition, he didn't seem like the type of man to judge another for simply surviving.

We'd just scoffed down the last of the omelet when I heard the front door open and close.

"Did you hear that?" I whispered, fork in air.

"Shall I go see who it is?" Penelope asked.

"That's not necessary," I said. It had to be Percival. No one else had a key. "It will be Dr. Bancroft, I suspect. Here to make sure I've settled in."

Sure enough, no sooner had I finished the sentence than Percival entered the kitchen with a bottle of wine in his hand. He abruptly stopped just inside the door. He blanched at the sight of us all around the kitchen table, then blinked as if he couldn't quite believe what he saw.

Feeling like a child caught stealing treats, I rose to my feet, my stomach fluttering with nerves. "Hello, Dr. Bancroft. Merry Christmas. I didn't expect to see you again today."

"It's Christmas, and I worried you might be lonely. I put Clara to bed, and Mother went to bed, so here I am." He nodded at Penelope and Mrs. Landry, who had also risen from the table. "Ladies."

They nodded at him, then started clearing the table, clearly unsure what to do next.

"This is my neighbor from across the hall," I said, introducing Percival to Joseph. "He was alone tonight too."

The men shook hands. Percival's expression resembled the one he'd had when he found me at the brothel. Jealousy mixed with rage.

"This has been wonderful, but I must go," Joseph said. "Thank you for the most enjoyable evening I've had in an age."

"You're very welcome," I said, returning his kind smile. "I'll be in touch about our idea."

"I can hardly wait," Joseph said.

Penelope rushed forward. "I'll show you out."

One last nod toward Percival and a quick glance at Mrs. Landry, and Joseph shot out of the kitchen rather like a ball bursting from a cannon.

"May I speak with you in the other room?" Percival asked tightly.

"Yes, of course. Thank you, Mrs. Landry, for the best omelet I've ever had," I said.

"My pleasure, Mrs. Wainwright."

With a heavy heart, I trudged out to the sitting room, with Percival not far behind. He still carried the bottle of wine, which Penelope noticed upon our arrival, offering to open it for us.

"No, thank you," Percival said. "I brought it as a gift for Stella."

"You may retire for the evening," I said to Penelope. "Thank you for keeping me company tonight."

"You're most welcome." She scuttled away, heading up the stairs to her room. I assumed Mrs. Landry would also retire in her sleeping quarters off the kitchen, leaving me alone with Percival.

He added another log to the fire before sitting in one of the wingback chairs.

"I didn't expect to see you again today," I said.

"As you said."

"What are you doing here?" I asked softly.

"To be honest, I'm not sure. Perhaps it was a mistake putting you in an apartment so close to mine. It's too easy to find myself walking here without consciously realizing I am doing so."

"I'll enjoy seeing you any time. We don't have to wait until Saturday."

"I was imagining you here all alone by the fire, feeling homesick or sad or whatever it is one feels on Christmas, but it was not the situation at all."

"Are you angry at me?" I asked timidly, despite my wish to appear brave and unaffected by his unexpected appearance. The truth was much different. I could hardly breathe, transfixed by his presence.

"No, not angry."

"Disappointed?"

"No. Not at all. Impressed, perhaps. And a little jealous, if I'm to be perfectly honest. I could hear your laughter the moment I walked in the door." His tone belied his words. He sounded tightly angry as if all his attention was concentrated on remaining civil.

"Oh, well…we were only making the best of what could have been a lonely evening. We're all without family."

"You have me," he said through gritted teeth.

"Only I don't. Not in the ways I wish. You know that. We agreed upon this arrangement."

He sighed, and all of the anger seemed to swoosh out of him, replaced by shame. "I know. After not seeing you for so long, having you back in my life is overwhelming. I cannot think of anything else. I'm tortured, knowing how close you are, yet how far away."

"I know," I whispered. "But it has to be this way."

"Yes."

"As far as the way I conduct myself, I see no reason why I cannot run my small staff as I see fit. If I'm to have little interaction with the outside world for fear of discovery, then I must form friendships within my tight circle. Surely you can understand the loneliness I face?"

He nodded, pinching the ridge of his nose between his thumb and middle finger. "Yes, I do. Of course, I do."

"Are you hungry?" I asked.

He retrieved his handkerchief from his pocket and wiped the debris left from the log from his hands. "No, we had a large supper. Mother insisted on goose, which I find greasy. But I do as she asks. As you know."

"Did Clara have a good rest of the day?" I asked, yearning for the sweet little girl I'd fallen for as deeply as I had Percival and his mother.

"Yes, she was spoiled rotten. I don't think it's good for the child to have so many toys, but Mother has no such worries."

"She's a well-behaved, kind girl, so whatever you're doing is working well. How's your mother?"

"She's in robust health as always. She told me to tell you hello and that she'd be by to see you soon."

"Did she know you were coming here tonight?"

"Yes. She knows everything," Percival said. "It's no use to try to hide anything from her."

I smiled, thinking of Mrs. Bancroft's strength of character and mighty will.

We sat in silence for a moment. It was unlike us, this quiet that hung so thickly in the air, holding all that we wished to say but could not.

"I should go," Percival said. "It's late, and you need your beauty rest."

"Yes, I suppose I do."

"I'll see you on Saturday?" Percival asked.

"I'm looking forward to it." I smiled.

"Yes. I'll pray you'll remain out of trouble until then?"

"I'll do my best."

I walked him to the door, shutting it behind him, wishing I could follow but knowing it was not to be.

2

___

PERCIVAL

On a morning three days after Christmas, I took the train up to see Mary at the asylum. The visit was uneventful. Of late, she seldom acknowledged my presence at all. The nurses said she had grown quiet the last few weeks. A depressive state, they'd called it, as opposed to the mania that she often exhibited.

I didn't stay long. As I left to take the train home, a deep melancholy made me heavy and weary. Was this to be my life? Weekly visits to a wife who no longer knew me while the woman I loved waited in an apartment like a caged bird?

By the time I arrived back to the city, it was nearing three. I decided not to go home straightaway but to take a walk in the park despite the chill in the air and the promise of snow. There were many people strolling or walking dogs, carriages full of merrymakers, and several food vendors with the scent of sausages filling the air. However, I barely registered anything, a crushing sadness like the blinders forced upon a horse, keeping my world insular.

When I arrived back at my home, I was dismayed to see that

Mary's brother Simon awaited me in my den. He sat by the fire, nursing a whiskey and reading a novel.

"Ah, there you are." He set aside his book on the nearest table. "Your mother said you'd be home an hour ago."

"I took a walk after I got off the train." I handed my coat and hat to Robert and joined my brother-in-law by the fire. "What brings you by?"

"Can't a brother stop by for a visit?"

"Yes, of course." I'd once welcomed his company, but anger over what he'd done to Stella had taken away any past warmth I felt for him. He'd forced my hand, which I didn't like. No man or woman liked to be manipulated for another's gain.

"How was my sister today?" Simon asked.

"Not one of her best days. She didn't know who I was, simply stared at the wall behind me."

He didn't comment or react, his face betraying no emotion.

"I've come from my gentleman's club," Simon said. "I heard something interesting. Something I must speak with you about."

"Yes?" Where was he going with this? Surely, he hadn't heard that I'd moved Stella into an apartment?

"Is it true? You've moved Miss Sullivan into an apartment?"

I didn't answer for a moment. My mind searched for an excuse, something to explain my decision without telling the exact truth. Which was I loved Stella. I could not have her the way I wished. However, I could not live with myself if I'd let her become a prostitute. She may not be my wife, but I'd decided without reservation that it was my duty to look after her. Seeing her in that world, I'd been desperate to keep her safe from ruin. And other men. I shuddered, thinking about any of them touching her.

I didn't pretend to understand why, but she felt like mine to take care of. If not me, then whom? Every man in her life had abandoned her at some point. I was not going to be the next one who betrayed her, letting her starve on the streets of New York

City or selling her body for survival. But how to explain this to my wife's brother? Impossible.

"I found her on Christmas Eve at Miss Scarlet's," I said. "Contemplating a life as a prostitute." He would know what I meant by Miss Scarlet. Any man in our circles knew Miss Scarlet ran a popular brothel.

Simon had the decency to flinch. "I see."

Anger flared deep in my belly. "You did it to her."

"She did it to herself."

"No, you made it happen. You ruined what was a good situation for her here with my mother and me. She had no place to go when we took her in. When you forced my hand—and I sent her away—she barely survived."

"How can you blame me? After what her family's done to mine? To ours?" Simon glared at me.

My brother-in-law had discovered a horrible connection between our families. In short, Stella's mobster father had put a hit out on Simon and Mary's father. A hit that sent Mr. Price to an early grave, followed soon thereafter by his wife. Simon believed that Mary's mental stability had been compromised because of it. Between the death of her parents and the psychosis that followed after the birth of our daughter Clara, my wife's sense of reality had been ruined. I'd been forced to put her in an asylum after she became too violent for me to take care of her properly. I'd feared for the safety of my mother and daughter, as well as for myself.

"I simply exposed Miss Sullivan for who she truly is," Simon said. "What happened to her after you very rightly sent her away is none of my concern. It should not be yours either. You're a married man."

"That's where you're wrong. She is my concern. She has no one but me. I will not let her die of poverty. For whatever reason, God put her in my path, and I cannot shirk my human responsibility toward a woman in need." I could still remember seeing her for the first time, wan from childbirth, the loneliness, and despair like a cloud around her. She'd needed me then, and she needed me now.

"That would be all good and well if you were not a married man," Simon said, his placid demeanor shifting slightly into hostility. "And if her family hadn't destroyed mine. Including sending my sister into madness."

"The sins of the father are not the sins of the child," I said, loosely quoting the Bible. "Anyway, what I do with an apartment I own is not for you to worry about. I've done right by your sister and will remain doing so for as long as she's alive. Surely you know that by now."

"Is Miss Sullivan your mistress?"

"She is my friend, nothing more. In addition, she'll be working with my mother as she was before your interference. She was doing a lot of good. It's not right to keep her from helping others."

"I don't like it," Simon said.

"I don't care."

Simon tossed back the remaining whiskey in his glass and stood. "The woman's trouble. If you cannot see that, then I cannot help you." He straightened his tie. "I'll show myself out."

After he left, I remained seated, staring into the fire, until Robert roused me from my stupor with an announcement of another visitor. "It's a boy named Stefano Rossi. Asking for the doctor. His little sister's very sick."

"Please have him wait in the foyer, out of the cold. It will take me a few minutes to gather my equipment."

"Yes sir," Robert said.

I rose to my feet, happy for the distraction, if not for the news of one of the Rossi children's falling ill. There were five children altogether, and they lived in one of the poorest sections of the city, where I spent a lot of my time giving free care to those in need. My medical degree did little to provide income, but it didn't matter. The inheritance from my father had set us up nicely, leaving me to carry out my life's purpose of caring for the destitute.

I asked one of the maids to fetch a fresh loaf of bread from our cook, as well as some slices of ham. The Rossi family could use them far more my own, I felt sure.

Clara, my six-year-old daughter, came running into the room, followed by her elderly nanny. They'd clearly been out for a walk. The cold air had stained Clara's cheeks the color of raspberries. Her dark curls bounced as she flew across the room to hurl herself into my arms. "Papa, we saw the most exciting thing in the park."

"And what is that?" I set her back onto the floor.

She gazed up at me, her nose wrinkling. "Are you going out? What about our game of checkers?"

I knelt, tugging locks of her hair behind her ears. "I'll be back soon. Little Maria Rossi is very sick, and I must tend to her." Between my mother's work and my own, Clara often heard us talk about the families we cared for. Like Mother, she had a great capacity for remembering details about people.

"Oh dear." Clara brought her hands to her mouth. "Will you be able to save her?"

"I hope so." I kissed the top of her glossy head and stood. "I'll be back as soon as I can."

"Papa, do you think they had presents at Christmas?" Her bottom lip trembled. "I've not thought of it until just now."

"I'm not sure, love."

She ran to the Christmas tree in the corner of the room and dropped to her knees, coming back to me with the checkers set I'd gotten her for Christmas.

"Papa, since we already have one, shouldn't we give this one to them?"

A lump developed in the back of my throat. It was true that we had another set, but it was worn and shabby, having first belonged to my father. Regardless, the game could be played just as easily on a worn board as a new one. "I think they would like that very much." This girl of mine had her grandmother's heart.

"Will they know how to play?" Clara asked, brow creasing.

"I'm sure they can learn. I must go now. I'll see you soon."

"Yes, Papa. Godspeed."

I stifled a smile. Godspeed? Where had she heard that?

A few minutes later, medical bag in hand, I followed young Stefano out to the street. My personal life might be in shambles, but providing medical care to the sick? This I could do.

STEFANO WAS the oldest of Mrs. Rossi's five children. At sixteen, he had taken on the role of father and provider after Mr. Rossi's death several years back. He didn't speak as my chauffeur, Joseph, drove us through the busy city streets until we reached Little Italy, where the Rossis lived.

Stefano and I hopped from the motorcar. I instructed Joseph to wait for me and then hurried through the battered tenement door, the dim light from the gas lamp flickering weakly in the cramped hallway. The narrow corridor, lined with peeling wallpaper and grime, smelled of mold mingled with the aroma of grease and the sharp tang of coal dust.

Stefano pushed open the creaking door. "Mama, I've got the doctor."

I stepped into the cramped living space. The room was dimly lit by a single flickering oil lamp. The scent of a thin stew simmering on the stove filled the air, barely masking the underlying smells of dampness and illness. The Rossi family's few possessions were neatly arranged and the room clean, despite the evident poverty.

Mrs. Rossi, her eyes shadowed with exhaustion, wore a

threadbare dress. Her once vibrant hair was tied back in a hasty bun. Despite her obvious fatigue, she offered me a grateful smile from where she sat by little Maria. "Thank you for coming, Dr. Bancroft," she said, her voice strained but warm. "I don't know what else to do. She's having trouble breathing."

The middle children, Antonio and Sofia, huddled together at the small rickety table, a shared schoolbook spread before them. Six-year-old Luca quietly played with a battered wooden train car near the corner of the room. Maria, the youngest, lay on a worn-out cot by the window, her small frame shivering under a thin blanket.

Setting the basket aside, I went to her, kneeling on the floor near her cot to get a better look. Maria's cheeks flushed with fever, and her eyes had a glassy look to them. Her breathing, indeed, sounded labored. When she coughed, a harsh, rattling sound came from deep in her chest.

I gently placed a hand on her forehead. The heat radiating from her skin was cause for alarm. Using my stethoscope, I listened to her lungs but detected no fluid. "Not pneumonia. Bronchitis, more likely."

"Thank God," Mrs. Rossi whispered.

For the next few minutes, I continued my examination. "I'd like you to soak some rags with water and hang them over the stove. She needs moisture in the air to help her lungs. Keep a cold compress on her forehead until the fever breaks." I took a bottle of acetylsalicylic acid from my bag and spoon-fed it into Maria's mouth to help reduce her fever. "You'll give her this every four hours. It should keep the fever from getting any higher." God willing. "Send Stefano to fetch me if there are any significant changes. Regardless, I'll come back to see her tomorrow morning."

I stood, remembering the food and gift I'd brought. "I've brought something from my mother." I put the loaf of bread and ham, wrapped in parchment paper, onto their rickety table.

"And this is from my daughter." I set the checkers game next to the food. "For the children."

"Please thank her for me," Mrs. Rossi said, wiping the corners of her eyes with the back of her hand.

As I stood to leave, I felt a tug on my coat. I looked down to see Luca gazing up at me with wide, frightened brown eyes.

"Is Maria dying, Dr. Bancroft?" Luca asked. "Like Papa?"

I knelt down, placing a hand on the boy's shoulder. "I certainly hope not. You help your mother look after her."

"I will, Dr. Bancroft," Luca said.

"I brought some treats in the basket for you," I said. "Make sure your mama eats some of it."

Luca nodded solemnly. "I'll try. Sometimes, she won't eat if she thinks we need it."

I set a hand on his shoulder. "Because she's a mother. That's what they do. But she needs her strength if she's to remain strong for all of you."

I bade them farewell and then walked down the hallway and out to the fresh, cold air. The previous day's snow lay over the ground and trees, sparkling in the bright sunlight. Joseph waited in the car, and I made haste, not wanting to disappoint my Clara.

SEVERAL BLOCKS FROM HOME, moving slowly through traffic, I spotted Stella walking along the sidewalk. At first, I thought she had her hands encased in a muff, but then realized she held a small black-and-white dog in her arms. Her head was bent over the dog, her mouth moving as if speaking with him. Where had she found him, and what was she doing with him? Then I noticed the man behind her. He kept pace with her, his gaze fixated on the back of her head but stayed about six feet behind. When she stopped to look in a window, he stopped. When she hesitated in front of a bakery, he hid behind a streetlamp, watching her. Narrowing my eyes, I took in the details of his personage. He wore a dark coat and top hat over silver hair.

Why would anyone be following Stella?

Many reasons.

Some of which might be explained by my earlier conversation with Simon. Did he have someone following her?

Or was it her father's doing? Had he discovered where she was and wanted to know more details of her life?

I couldn't explain it, but something told me there was something nefarious afoot. Was she in danger, and if so, why?

"Please, pull over," I said to Joseph.

He did as I asked, moving out of traffic to come to a stop next to Stella. I leaned my head out of the car. "Stella, here." I waved my hand to get her attention.

The moment I did, the man in the top hat shuffled off in the other direction. I knew it.

Upon seeing me, Stella's eyes widened, and a smile spread over her face. "Percy?" She walked toward the car, still holding the dog. When she reached me, she nodded toward the mutt with her chin, a delighted sparkle in her eyes. "I found a dog. He's skinny and dirty but very sweet."

More concerned over her than the dog, I merely nodded. He was a scruffy little thing with matted fur and dirty paws. I spoke without moving my lips. "Do not react, but there was a man following you. He may still be watching. Or there may be others."

"I don't understand."

"Please get in the car with me. Don't make a fuss. Act as if I meant to come pick you up."

"Yes, all right."

When she and the dog were settled next to me, I asked Joseph to take us to her apartment. "You'll leave me there and return home."

"Yes, Dr. Bancroft," Joseph said.

"Are you sure someone was following me?" Stella held tight to the dog despite his muddy paws staining her coat.

"Quite sure."

Soon we were at the entrance of her apartment building. I helped her and the mangy mutt out of the car and into the building. Benny, the doorman, greeted us with a friendly smile.

"Good afternoon, Dr. Bancroft. Mrs. Wainwright."

"Good afternoon," I said.

"What have we here?" Benny peered into the lump of fluff in Stella's arms.

"I found him in an alleyway," Stella said. "He's starved."

"Indeed," Benny said. "May I help in any way?"

"No, I'm going to take him upstairs and bathe him," Stella said. "And feed him, obviously."

"Yes, Mrs. Wainwright. Very wise, I'd say." Benny signaled to the elevator operator to escort us upstairs.

By the time we reached the floor of Stella's apartment, I'd decided this was not only a mangy little mutt but a smelly one too.

3

ESTELLE

By the time Penelope and I had given the dog a bath, dried him with a towel, and given him a scrap or two from last night's supper, Percival was in a powerful snit.

Penelope had brought out a stack of old blankets for the dog's bed, which we put near the fire.

"Take a little rest," I said to the dog as I put him onto the makeshift bed. Thus far, he hadn't barked, only whined or whimpered. His tail wagged before he curled up into a ball and went to sleep. I gave him one last scratch behind the ears before facing Percival.

"Tell me everything," Percival said, turning from where he stood by the window.

"Yes, well, what happened is—I was walking back from the dressmaker, who was absolutely lovely and very efficient. Please thank your mother for making the appointment. She's making three new day dresses and two evening gowns. I won't need them unless I'm invited somewhere, but your mother had given her instruction to make both. I don't know why, but it was thoughtful of her."

"You needed new dresses, and Mother knows what to do, so I asked her to communicate our needs," Percival said, shrugging as if it were of no consequence. "Anyway, when you left the shop, what happened?"

"I heard this cry, almost like a human baby." I shuddered, the sounds of my baby's cries haunting me until I pushed the thought aside. "And I looked into the alley, and there he was. Just curled into a miserable ball. I had to bring him home. What kind of person just left him like that?"

"Stella, as much as I admire your big heart, I don't care about the dog. Not right now, at least."

"What?" My mouth fell open. "Not care about the dog? How do you mean?"

"I want to know about the man who was following you."

"Oh, well. Are we sure he really was? Following me, that is?"

"I'm certain."

"But who would care about me?" Who could have sent someone to follow me? My father? Simon? Someone else?

"You didn't notice him?" Percival asked.

"No. I'm sorry."

Percival rubbed his eyes. "I'm not going to sleep tonight."

"I'm safe here. Benny won't let anyone get to me." Our doorman seemed the conscientious sort and had clearly taken a liking to me.

"Unless they hurt him to get to you."

That hit me hard. So hard my legs went numb. I sank into a chair. "Do you think it's my father?" I whispered, too horrified at the thought to say it any louder. Why would he follow me? What could he want from me? Other than to know where I lived? Did he want to see me?

Percival was pacing around the room, stopping occasionally to peek out the window. "I've no idea. I want you to stay inside for now. I'm sorry, but until I know what's happening, I don't want you out and about."

"What about him?" I gestured toward the dog. "He'll need to go outside to...you know."

"Perhaps Penelope can take him?"

"What if they try to hurt her to get to me? I couldn't bear it if anything happened to her." Penelope had been such a loyal companion and friend. She deserved better than to be harmed because of me.

"Yes, you're right." Percival sat across from me, spreading his hands over his knees. "Here's what we're going to do. I'll hire a bodyguard to keep watch on your apartment. Anyone suspicious, he'll take care of."

I swallowed. "By take care of—you mean...?"

"I don't know." Percival ran a hand through his hair, sounding cross and harassed.

"Percival, I don't think a bodyguard is necessary. I'll stay inside."

"I want you to stay inside, yes. But I'm hiring someone to keep watch over you. Also, you must send Penelope out for errands. Just until we know who this is and what they want."

"All I've done since you found me on the train is cause you trouble. I'm sorry."

He lifted his gaze to meet mine. "You needn't apologize. None of this has been your fault."

I took in a deep breath, hoping to calm my muddled thoughts. "Perhaps my father discovered the connection between you and me. Could it have made him worried that I would discover the truth about what he did to your family and wants to make sure I remain quiet?"

Percival nodded. "Moving in here may have alerted him to our connection, I suppose."

"Or maybe he thinks I know where Mauve and Pierre went? They left for France soon after I came to the city. Could he be trying to find them? For Mother? She lost us all at once." I'd not spent much time thinking about my mother since I'd fled. My anger toward her might have been the strongest of all. How did a mother allow her husband to do what he'd done to me and to Mauve? If he hadn't had Constantine killed, we would be married now. Mireille would be with me and not my twin. Everything in my life would be different.

But as I'd learned over and over since Connie's death, I could no longer dream of what could have been and instead must accept what is.

"Have you received any letters from your sister?" Percival asked.

I flushed with shame. "No. I promised to write, but I haven't. She and Pierre have no idea where I am other than here in the city. Pierre took them to his family's vineyard in Bordeaux."

"You have the address?" Percival asked. "Why didn't you write to them?"

"I-it's hard to explain."

"Try."

"There are two reasons. Firstly, I'm ashamed of what's become of me."

Percival flinched but made no comment.

"Secondly, when I dig deep within myself, examining what is right and what is best for all involved, it is for me to remain absent from Mireille's life. Pierre and Mauve deserve to raise Mireille as their own, without ghosts from the past confusing her."

"They might have been able to help you. Financially, that is."

"No, Pierre's family's not wealthy. They would not have anything to spare."

"And you're too proud to ask," Percival said.

I didn't answer, merely nodded as tears filled my eyes. "It's too painful to hear about her and not be there to witness any of it."

He leaned closer, taking my hand for a moment and just as

quickly dropping it. "I wish I could take your pain away. I would if I could."

I looked into his sympathetic eyes. "I know."

"I'm going to talk to Simon. I don't believe he's behind this, but I want to make sure. Having you followed gives him nothing. He already knows where you are." He stood. "In the meantime, please stay inside." He gestured toward the dog. "I'm assuming you're keeping him?"

"Where else would he go?" Like me, he didn't have a lot of choices. "He doesn't have anyone, obviously. We fit together that way."

"You have me."

Not in the way I wanted, but I nodded in agreement, forcing a smile. "Yes, and I'm grateful."

"Please, try and stay out of trouble. I leave you alone, and look what's happened." Percival smiled, gesturing toward the sleeping dog. "Are you sure you want him to stay?"

"More than anything."

"Fine. But I am sincere in asking you to please ask Penelope to take him out."

"I promise. But is it possible you're overreacting just a small amount?"

"If I am, then so be it," Percival said. "I want you to be safe. That's all."

"Thank you." I touched the sleeve of his jacket. "I appreciate your concern."

I walked Percival to the door and closed it behind him, listening to his steps as he made his way down the hallway.

Penelope, who had been hiding in the kitchen, came out to see if I needed anything.

"No, I'm fine," I told her about the man following me and Percival's worry. "He's sending a man over to guard the door."

"We can't be too safe, I'd imagine," Penelope said.

"I suppose not."

An hour or so later, Percival returned with a young man by his side. "This is Henry. He'll keep a close watch," Percival said.

"It's a pleasure to meet you, Henry." I flushed, embarrassed by his presence. This was too much. Or was it? My father had killed Connie and Mr. Price. He clearly had no loyalty to me, but would he actually physically harm me? If it was indeed Father. I still hadn't ruled out my nemesis, Simon Price. But honestly, I felt tired and numb without an anchor.

At least I was warm and fed. I must remember to be grateful.

"At night, he'll stay outside your door, ensuring no one gets in," Percival said.

Henry had a broad face, floppy blond curls, and big blue eyes. Percival, who wasn't a small man himself, looked dwarfed next to the wide-shouldered, broad Henry. Where had he found him?

"Henry has worked as a guard in several capacities," Percival explained. "He comes highly recommended."

"Thank you, Dr. Bancroft," Henry said. "I'll do my best to keep them safe from harm."

"I must go," Percival said. "I have a patient to look in on, so I must go."

In all the excitement, I'd almost forgotten.

"I'll return after dark," Henry said to me. "I'll be right outside your door. Please don't hesitate to ask if you need anything at all."

"May I speak with you?" I asked Percival. "Alone."

Henry excused himself, leaving me to face Percival.

"A bodyguard is completely unnecessary," I said. "I promised you I'd be careful."

He ran both hands through his hair. "If anything were to happen to you—I couldn't stand it. Please, humor me. Let me do this."

"Yes, all right, but I think it's a silly way to spend your money."

"Let me be the judge of that," he said. "Now, I must go."

I watched him walk out the door, wishing it wasn't so. I wanted to be with him, safe in his arms, not at the mercy of a guard standing outside my apartment.

I spent the rest of the day with the dog, encouraging him to sit on my lap while I stroked his adorable head.

When I was a kid, I'd asked for a dog, but Mother had not thought it was a good idea. Since then, I'd promised myself that when I was grown and married, I'd get one or two. That had seemed impossible until today. I had an apartment and plenty of food to share with him. Perhaps he would help me to feel less lonesome at night.

"You'll need a name," I said as I put him on the end of my bed that night. "What shall it be?" I folded a blanket and set him on top of it, hoping he would understand that if he were to be up here, he must remain by my feet.

He'd yet to make a sound other than a whine or a soft snore when he was asleep in the basket, and he made none now.

"You're certainly not a barker, are you?"

His ears twitched.

"What's a name for a quiet boy like you?" I searched my memory for what I would have named a dog if I'd been able to have one as a kid and the name Charlie popped into my mind. "How about Charlie? Is that a good name for a sweet boy like you?"

His tail wagged, and I could swear he was smiling at me.

"Charlie, welcome home."

He pushed his wet nose against my hand, and I pulled him close for one last snuggle before setting him onto the blanket at the end of the bed.

Soon, we were both settled in for the night. I yawned, nestling into my pillow. Percival had been correct. I felt much safer knowing Henry was outside my door.

As for Charlie? He would not be much of a watchdog, but I didn't care. He was perfect just the way he was.

THE NEXT MORNING, I was awakened by movement at the end of my bed. I sat up, rubbing my eyes, before remembering that I'd brought home a new friend.

"Good morning, Charlie," I said.

He sat on his haunches, watching me with his button-shaped brown eyes. I patted the spot next to me, and he trotted up to sit by me. After a good rub of his ears and belly, I reached for my dressing gown and got out of bed.

Penelope knocked and called out to me before stepping inside with a tray, holding my morning coffee and a roll. Fully dressed, with her hair pulled back neatly at the nape of her neck, she appeared as efficient and cheerful as always. "Good morning, Miss Stella. I've successfully found a leash for the dog. Shall I take him out for you?"

"Yes, but please, be mindful of your surroundings. Dr. Bancroft wants us to pay attention while we're out, just in case he's correct that someone wants to do me harm."

"I will indeed." Penelope picked the pup up off the bed. "What are you naming him?"

"Charlie. I don't know why, but it seems to suit him."

Penelope grinned. "Hello, Charlie. Shall we go outside and then have some breakfast?"

Charlie wagged his tail in agreement.

"You may tell Henry he can go home and get some rest," I said. "We should be fine as long as I stay inside."

After they left, I poured myself a cup of coffee and went to the window. Drawing the curtains back, I looked down to the street. Soon, Penelope appeared with Charlie on the leash. I watched as they walked toward the park, looking this way and that to see if I could spot the man from the day before. The street and sidewalks were busy already, teeming with folks on their way to church or out for strolls. Motorcars made their way along the street, flinging muddy snow from their tires.

I saw nothing out of the ordinary. Had Percival seen something that wasn't there? Who could blame him after all that had transpired between our two families.

Later, Penelope fixed my hair and helped me dress for the day. It was hard to understand all the ways my life had changed since leaving home. Ups and downs were part of life, but mine seemed to be in the extreme.

Mrs. Bancroft arrived around ten that morning, bringing a stack of books. I'd not seen her since I'd left her home months before, but I was not prepared for the well of emotion that flooded me. She'd become like a mother to me in the time I spent at their home. I'd felt understood and cherished under her care. When Simon exposed who I really was to Percival and his mother, I'd faced yet another loss. Now, however, she stood before me, rosy-cheeked and smiling.

"Dear girl, it's wonderful to see you."

Penelope took the books from her and set them on a table, then helped her out of her coat.

Mrs. Bancroft held out her hands, and I took them, tears stinging my eyes. "How have you been?" I asked.

"Well, although I've missed you terribly. We have a lot to discuss."

"Shall I bring tea?" Penelope asked.

"Yes, please," I said before ushering Mrs. Bancroft over to sit near the hearth.

Charlie, who had been asleep by the fire, lifted his head in greeting.

"What is this?" Mrs. Bancroft asked. "Or, rather, who is this?"

"Percival didn't tell you? I found a dog. I've named him Charlie."

"Percy was too worried about everything else, I guess, to mention it," Mrs. Bancroft said. "He's a cute little thing."

As if in agreement, Charlie placed his chin on his paws and looked up at us.

"He'll be good company," Mrs. Bancroft said. "Have you been lonely?"

"No, I've been fine. I have the staff here, so it's not bad. Not at all. I'm lucky to be here."

"I'm glad to know you're safe now. I worried myself sick after you left. I'd have gone after you if I'd had any inclination of where you might have gone."

"I'm sorry to worry you."

"No, we're the ones who let you down," Mrs. Bancroft said.

"How is Clara?"

"She's well. We had a quiet but joyous Christmas."

I wanted to ask if the child ever asked about me, but I didn't want to make her uncomfortable. Clara was only six. She'd likely forgotten all about me.

"Where do we begin?" Mrs. Bancroft asked.

"I've no idea."

"I shall start, then. I'd like you to know that whatever crimes and atrocities your father committed, they are his alone, not yours. What he's done—it in no way influences my opinion of you."

"He killed Connie," I blurted out.

"Yes, I'm aware. In fact, I've done some investigating of my own into your father and Mary's as well. It appears they have much in common. Unfortunately."

Penelope arrived with our tea and a plate of cinnamon cakes. We thanked her before resuming our conversation.

"Have you discovered anything I should know?" My voice shook. I wanted to know but didn't at the same time. How was that possible? To be brave and terrified in conjunction?

"Apparently, they were rivals over territories. Your father ordered the hit on him, as you know."

"Yes. Setting in motion Mary's demise," I said. "Making my family responsible for Percival's unhappiness. And poor Clara without a mother."

"I don't think we can blame it all on the war between mobsters. She was always fragile. You mustn't take any blame upon your own shoulders."

"Thank you. I find that difficult."

"I understand." She hesitated, taking a sip of tea. "That's all I know, which isn't more than you already did. I thought I might discover some new truth, but it is as we thought. However, if it's true that someone's been hired to follow you, then we might have further troubles. I know it will be hard to stay inside, but Percival's most likely right about what he saw yesterday."

"Thus the books?"

"Correct. I thought you might need something to do. It's a shame, as I was looking forward to having you back by my side. The last few months have been lonely. I'd not realized how much I'd come to rely on you until after you were gone. You surprised me, not only with your ability to learn quickly but your tenacity in keeping up with me."

"Thank you. I'm humbled." Her words pleased me no end. She found me useful and a quick learner? This gave me something warm to hold on to during the chaos that had become my life.

"Percy's hired someone to look into the man following you—to figure out if it *is* your father who has hired someone to watch you."

"It has to be," I said. "He's discovered where I am and wants to make sure I won't go to the police with what I know. There can be no other explanation."

"Other than Simon."

"Yes, of course." Simon. How I wished he'd never returned from Europe.

"I've been thinking through that possibility and have come up with nothing. What possible motive could he have? Is he disturbed that Percy's taking care of you? Yes. But I don't think there's anything he's trying to prevent. He has no ties to illegal acts, thus, I see no reason for him to have you followed."

"He's protective of his sister," I said. "Percival's friendship with me disturbs him."

"Yes, but still. Why would he have you followed? What happens between these walls he is not privy to."

I flushed with heat at her implication.

"Now, none to that," Mrs. Bancroft said. "I know you and Percival have vowed to remain friends only. It's a shame."

Simply too mortified to respond, I kept silent, perspiration dampening the palms of my hands. Mrs. Bancroft clearly had different ideas about morality than her son. Or me, for that matter. Had age changed her? Exposed her to enough hurt and disappointment from her own marriage and subsequent years alone that things no longer seemed as simple as they once had? Did she see the world in shades of gray? Her only son faced a lonely life without any chance for another love or marriage. As long as his wife remained alive, he was bound to her. I knew she wished only for Percival and Clara to be happy and loved. With the current situation, they would not have the love of a wife or mother. Unless a miracle happened, and Mary suddenly became well?

The thought of that made it hard to breathe. I was a terrible person, wishing that she remain ill so that I could continue living here. But the realities of what I'd faced before Percival rescued me were still fresh in my mind. Cold New York winters without shelter or food? They would have been my future.

"Did Percival tell you where he found me on Christmas

Eve?" I had to ask. Not knowing would make it more difficult than just facing up to the truth.

"He did." She reached over the table and took my hand in both of hers. "I don't blame you or judge you. How could I, when there by the grace of God go I? I'm thankful he found you. I shudder to think what you would have had to endure had you stayed."

"You're a remarkable woman, Mrs. Bancroft," I said.

She waved her hand dismissively. "Stop that. I'm neither good nor bad. I want only for those I love to be free and happy. Anyway, I must go. I've several families to call on today, and I have to be home early to prepare for a party."

A few minutes later, Mrs. Bancroft was gone—off to do her work. I couldn't help but feel bereft upon her departure. I yearned to do something good and decent. After the kindness shown me, I felt a compulsion to give it to others.

But it would seem my father would ruin that too.

4

PERCIVAL

Mother and I had been invited to a dance at the Ashfords' for New Year's Eve. I'd not planned on attending, but Mother mentioned Simon would be there. Since I wanted to talk to him, I decided to don my tuxedo and join my mother.

On the ride over in our motorcar, with Joseph driving, Mother glanced at me occasionally, clearly worried about something.

Finally, I decided to address whatever was bothering her. "What is it?" I asked gently. "You have that look in your eyes."

She sighed and clasped her white-gloved hands in her lap. "You've been distracted and distant. Is there anything you'd like to talk about?"

I gestured discreetly at Joseph, who I had no doubt listened to everything we said. I'd grown distrustful of him over the last few days. He'd been outright rude to Stella when I'd brought her up to the apartment for the first time. Since then, he'd not made eye contact with me, even when I addressed him directly. Or I might be growing paranoid.

"I'll speak with you later." I placed my hand over hers and gave them a squeeze. "But please don't worry. I'm fine."

Joseph, despite my reservations, expertly navigated the bustling streets until the Ashfords' impressive mansion came into view. We drove down the long driveway, lined with perfectly manicured hedges and marble lion statues.

"Oh, it looks lovely, doesn't it?" Mother asked.

I glanced at her, surprised. She was not typically impressed by the opulence of the extremely wealthy. Perhaps it was because she'd been shunned so often by the elite. Or perhaps it was her lack of interest that caused her to be excluded from many events in New York society. Either way, I'd always been grateful I had a good excuse to avoid parties such as this. However, Mother had recently met the new Mrs. Ashford, the second wife to John Ashford and thirty years his junior, during a fundraiser. Although they were of different ages and circumstance, my mother and Mrs. Ashford had bonded over their shared passion for philanthropy. Thus, we'd received an invite to what was supposed to be the party of the holiday season.

As Joseph pulled the motorcar up to the entrance, a doorman in a sharp uniform stepped forward, opening Mother's car door. While he helped her to the ground, I got out the other side. The cold air hit my face as strains of jazz music and the soft murmur of conversation and laughter drifted from the mansion.

The driveway and entrance bustled with activity, with well-dressed men and women being escorted inside. We followed a group of people up steps lined with lush red carpet and flanked by wrought iron railings. Uniformed staff were stationed along the way, ready to assist and guide guests into the mansion.

Once inside the grand foyer, a courteous attendant took our coats and hats. I looked around, taking in the high ceilings, sparkling chandeliers, and richly decorated walls. They'd spared no expense. Good for them, I supposed.

Our hosts, Mr. and Mrs. Ashford, stood near the entrance, graciously greeting each guest. Mrs. Ashford, young and beautiful, was dressed in an elegant pink gown. Her dark hair had been twisted into an elaborate hairstyle that mimicked the shorter cuts of some of the women.

"Mrs. Bancroft, how good of you to come." Mrs. Ashford kissed both of Mother's cheeks before introducing us to her husband. He looked considerably older, with a shock of white hair and a thick mustache.

"Thank you for coming. Enjoy yourselves," Mr. Ashford said before turning to address a man he clearly had more interest in than us.

As we headed down the hallway to the grand ballroom, the sounds of jazz music grew louder. We stepped through the doorway to a large room adorned with crystal chandeliers, which cast a warm, glittering light over the polished marble floors. The walls were decorated with intricate gold leaf details and rich, deep-hued tapestries.

Women wore dresses made of silk and chiffon, embellished with beads and sequins that caught the light as they moved about. Some had their hair styled in sleek bobs, others in elegant updos, adorned with feathers, pearls, and jeweled headbands. Men were dressed in impeccably tailored tuxedos, with crisp white shirts and black bow ties.

The band, complete with a grand piano, brass instruments, and a lively drum set, played a lively jazz tune. Couples danced to the happy tune, clearly enjoying themselves.

A team of waitstaff circulated the room, offering guests champagne in crystal flutes or taking their order for a crafted cocktail. The bar featured an impressive display of spirits and mixers, with bartenders skillfully preparing drinks.

"What can I get you, Mother?"

"Shall we eat something?"

"Yes, wonderful idea," I said.

A waiter appeared, offering us a glass of champagne, but I asked if he might point us in the direction of the food.

"Food is being served in the conservatory," the waiter said. "Please allow me to escort you?"

We followed him out of the ballroom and down the hallway to the conservatory. Made of glass walls and ceiling, exotic plants, and comfortable seating arrangements, the room offered a serene escape from the bustling ballroom.

Long tables were laden with an array of hors d'oeuvres, seafood platters, slices of beef, an entire roasted pig, and decadent desserts. Guests helped themselves to generous plates, dining at small tables and plush sofas arranged around the room.

Mother and I followed suit, soon finding our way to a small table with plates filled with food.

"Do you know any of these people?" I asked under my breath.

"A few look familiar, but not really."

I ate in silence until I'd had enough. No sooner had I pushed my plate aside than a waiter came to clean up after me. Mother was swept away by a few of her suffragette friends, leaving me alone. Another bar had been set up in here, so I wandered over and ordered a gin rickey, then sat on one end of a recently abandoned sofa.

This was going to be a long night.

I'd almost finished my drink when I saw Simon enter the conservatory. He was alone and seemed to quickly notice me as he strode my direction.

I stood to greet him. "Simon, I didn't know you were here." Somehow, I kept my anger and suspicion from infiltrating my voice.

"It was a last-minute decision to attend. May I sit?"

"Sure. I know almost no one here," I said. If only I'd had a wife to smooth out my rougher edges and help me to mingle. Alas, I would rather have been home with a book, and that fact no doubt showed in my demeanor. Regardless, I was glad Simon found me. If he were the one who'd had Stella followed, then I wanted to know.

Unsure how to start, I simply blurted out what I wanted to say. "Someone's following Stella. Did you hire someone?"

He appeared baffled for a moment before answering. "What? Why would I do that?"

"The same reason you investigated her in the first place."

"I have no interest in her whatsoever, other than she's a threat to our family. You're aware she's a liar, aren't you? Why are you surprised she's being followed? Who knows what kinds of thugs she's involved with."

As much as I hated to admit it, he had a point. Although, we differed in our opinions on one primary point. Nothing that had happened had been Stella's fault. She was innocent. Her father was the villain here. I couldn't understand how Simon didn't see that. Or wouldn't.

I was about to get up and leave him when a waiter hurried over with a note on a tray. "For you, Dr. Bancroft."

"Who's it from?" I asked.

"I'm not certain, Dr. Bancroft. It was brought to me from one of the men parking motorcars. He said a woman dropped it off for you."

I stood, thanking him as I retrieved the envelope with my name written in loopy handwriting on it. "If you'll excuse me, Simon, I must read this in private." That wasn't entirely true, as I had no idea who it was from. I did, however, desire greatly to leave my brother-in-law's company.

I found a quiet spot in the home's library in which to open the envelope. To my great surprise, it was from Miss Scarlet. This could only mean one thing. She had information on Stella's father. When I negotiated Stella's release from the brothel, I'd asked Miss Scarlet to keep her ears and eyes open. Should Sean

Sullivan appear at a party, she'd promised to gather as much intelligence as possible. In exchange for a fee, of course. Miss Scarlet was a businesswoman, after all.

Dear Dr. Bancroft,

Please forgive the intrusion, but I received word of your attendance at the Ashfords' party this evening. I have information I believe you'll be interested to hear. If possible, please come by tonight so that I might share with you what I learned.

Sincerely,

Miss Scarlet

I FOLDED the note and slid it back into the envelope, then put it in the inner pocket of my dinner jacket. This was as good an excuse as any to abandon the festivities. I'd pretend to have a headache and ask Simon to see Mother home.

Simon agreed without reservation to look after Mother. Clearly not believing I truly had a headache, he could not keep the curiosity from his eyes. Regardless, he let me go without question. Hopefully, he would not follow me.

I found Mother sitting in the music room with a few of her friends. She looked up at me as I entered.

"Ladies." I bowed my head in their direction. "I'm terribly sorry, but could I steal my mother away for a few minutes?"

They all nodded politely. I drew Mother over to an empty corner of the room, looking around to make sure we would not be heard by any curious gossip seekers.

"What is it? Is Stella all right?"

"Yes, she's fine. As far as I know, anyway. I have word from

Miss Scarlet. She has information for me, thus, I'm going to see her now. Simon will see you home."

Her eyes registered disappointment, but she quickly stifled it. "Of course, dear. I'll see you in the morning, then?"

"Yes, after calling on Miss Scarlet, I'm going home straight away. This isn't my kind of event."

"I know, and I thank you for at least staying as long as you did."

"Good night, Mother. I'll see you tomorrow. Joseph will be here at midnight to take you and Simon home."

"I shall not be late nor lose my slipper."

"See that you don't, Cinderella." I kissed Mother's cheek and then scurried out to the hallway before I could be waylaid by another guest.

After retrieving my coat and hat, I went out to the dark night. Although the weather was cold, with occasional flakes of icy snow falling upon my nose, I decided to walk to Miss Scarlet's. The fresh air would do me good. The streets were quiet, with only a few motorcars and trolleys taking people to their destinations.

I didn't see them coming. I'd just rounded the corner of the block where Miss Scarlet's infamous dwelling was lit up with its usual debauchery when two men, both wearing masks, pulled me into an alley. They were large, tall, and wide. One slammed my head against the side of the brick building. The other punched me in the gut. Next thing I knew, I was on the ground, and a heavy boot kicked my stomach.

"What do you want?" I managed to get out before another blow, this time to my back, rendered me temporarily mute. "I've money. Take all of it."

"We don't want your money. We're delivering a message from Mr. Sullivan."

Mr. Sullivan. Stella's father. Had Miss Scarlet set me up? Invited me to come by while these two lay in wait?

"What is it?" I asked.

"He wants you to stay away from his daughter," the taller of the two said as he yanked me to my feet.

I knew I should just agree and hope they left me to nurse my wounds. But I couldn't do it. Not when it came to Stella. "He shouldn't have tossed her into the streets if he wanted me to stay away from her."

The man who so far had not spoken shoved me back into the wall. "She's not your concern."

"Then whose concern is she? Her family's abandoned her. I'm simply providing her a safe place to live."

"Mr. Sullivan don't like it."

"Why?" I had to ask.

"Because of the connection between your two families. You want to keep Miss Sullivan and your mother safe? Then send her away."

"Not to mention that pretty little daughter of yours." The creepy edge to his voice sent blood through my veins.

Rage like no other made my legs shake, and my chest constrict. "You stay away from my daughter."

His hands went around my neck. "You stupid or something? You're not in charge here. Mr. Sullivan's a very powerful man. You can't fight him and hope to win. You really want your mother and daughter harmed because you chose the wrong mistress? Do you want that on your conscience?"

"She's not my mistress," I muttered.

"Yeah, right. 'Cause men just put a female acquaintance up in one of the finest buildings in New York City? Do I look like a fool, Dr. Bancroft?"

"I can't see your face, so I'm not sure I can answer that." I knew I was playing with fire, but these two had angered me beyond reason.

In response to my sarcasm, the palm of his hand slammed

my head against the brick, this time hard enough, I saw bright dots of light play before my eyes.

"Should we kill him for fun?" Glittering black eyes peered out from the holes in the mask, catching the light from the street. His stale breath felt warm on my skin.

"Nah, not tonight. Boss said to send the message first and give him time to respond accordingly."

My heart beat fast and heavy. I had to get out of here alive. I had three women who needed me. Four if I counted Mary, I thought shamefully. "Whatever happened between Mr. Sullivan and my father-in-law has nothing to do with me or Miss Sullivan. We have no interest in revisiting...that time."

"Simon Price has been nosing around, looking into things he ain't supposed to. You get me?" For the first time, I detected a hint of an Italian accent.

"As a matter of clarity, I do not understand," I said softly.

"You tell your brother-in-law, if he values his life, to let this go. Mr. Sullivan can't have busybodies going to the police and stirring things up."

My mind raced and raced, trying to pinpoint exactly what was going on here. Simon had gone to the police? About his suspicions that Sullivan had killed his father? What was Simon doing? Trying to get himself killed?

"I'll tell him," I said. "I'll get him to back off. Please, don't hurt my family. Tell Mr. Sullivan that neither I nor his daughter know anything about her father's business enterprises. We just want to be left alone. My wife's not well, as I'm sure you know. I don't need any further trouble."

"Yeah, that's a shame. She must take after her old man. Violent and not right in the head, you know what I mean?"

That had never occurred to me.

"Mr. Price should understand that the police are friends to Mr. Sullivan," the talkative thug said. "Making him untouchable."

"Yes, all right. I'll get Simon to back off," I said.

"See that you do." He released his hands from around my neck, and he and his partner sprinted down the alleyway and disappeared around the building.

For a moment I simply stood there, shaking and sweaty, trying to gather my thoughts. I would not go inside to speak with Miss Scarlet, as I felt sure she'd sent me the note in order to get me to come over. Not that I had previously, but this proved she was not to be trusted.

Mother. She and Simon were supposed to leave together. They were vulnerable, alone in a car with Joseph. Any number of things could happen on these icy streets. Things that could be made to look like an accident.

I took off running. Back to the Ashfords' to find my mother and escort her home myself.

A RISING panic made it hard to think, but I managed to get back to the party, collect Simon and Mother, and bring them home. Because I wanted to talk to Simon, I asked that he come in with us. Joseph would wait for him on the street and take him back to his own apartment once I was done.

Mother had not stopped fretting since she saw my face, which I'm sure looked swollen and purple by this time. My head ached, and my stomach felt as if a heavy boot had smashed into me, which, of course, it had.

"Percy, what's going on? You have me scared to death," Mother said as she took a seat on the sofa. Simon sat in one of the chairs, looking at me as if he knew what I was going to say. That might have terrified me most of all.

"Yes, I'm sorry. This won't take long." I collapsed onto the other end of the sofa and drew in a deep breath. "Something happened after I left the party." As precisely as I could, I described the event as I remembered it.

Mother's hands flew to her mouth and stayed there through my explanation. Simon merely looked at me through glittering eyes.

"What's Sullivan so afraid of?" Simon asked when I was finished. "That we'll prove he killed my father?"

"I believe so. Primarily because you keep poking around. Going to the police, if that's what you did, has only made it worse. I'm sure the police department's in his pocket. Anything you do or ask gets back to Sullivan."

"You've been to the police?" Mother asked Simon. "What did you think that would do other than draw attention to our family?"

Simon let his head drop into his hands for a second before speaking. "I don't know. It was stupid. In hindsight, I can see that. I'm angry. So very angry. I can't seem to let it go."

"These are mobsters, Simon," I said. "They won't hesitate to kill us all. I'm begging you, please, stop whatever it is you're doing."

"What about Stella?" Mother asked. "Is she in danger, too?"

"Yes. I have the guard outside her apartment, but the minute she steps out, she could be hurt or worse. There's no doubt in my mind that the man following her was sent by her father. He must think she's working with us. The coincidence that we met on a train, although true, would seem impossible to him. He wants to know what she's doing with me."

"Would he hurt his own daughter?" Mother asked.

"I don't know," I said. "He killed Stella's fiancé and then tossed her away like trash. Those are not the actions of a benevolent man."

"This is my fault," Simon said. "When I discovered who Miss Sullivan was, it brought everything up again. I lie awake at night, dreaming of revenge. He took my entire family from me. It's not something I can easily forget."

"No one's asking you to," I said. "But you must accept that Sean Sullivan's a powerful and violent gangster, and he wants us to go away, one way or another."

"Yes, I can see that clearly now. I have a friend in the police department. I asked him to my club and told him what I knew." Simon hesitated, shifting in his chair. "I asked him to look into it."

I pushed aside my anger. Although Simon should have known better, the compulsion for justice had outweighed his logic. In addition to Simon's father's death, Sean Sullivan had indeed been a factor in the decline of my wife. I felt sure of that, although we could never prove it.

"I'm sorry," Simon said. "I had no idea he was dirty."

"What do we do now?" Mother asked, voice trembling.

"The men who beat me up told me I had to get Simon to stop asking questions. I think if we do that, they'll leave us alone. If not, we're all in danger. Even Clara."

"Simon, what were you thinking?" Mother asked. "This man killed your father over a turf war. Do you really think he didn't know the risk when he started running illegal businesses? This is as much his fault as it is Sullivan's. Can you accept that this is a fight between bad men and leave us out of it? Haven't you suffered enough?"

Simon nodded, looking defeated. "You're right. I suppose I had fantasies of taking down the entire crime world, but that was clearly ridiculous. I want someone to pay for...my mother and Mary mostly. And it's true, he's as much to blame as Sullivan. There's no one to whom I can direct my anger and my need for vengeance. Not if it puts us in harm's way." He dropped his face into his hands for a moment before returning his gaze to mine. "I'll go back to Europe. That'll show them I'm out of the way."

"I hate to see you go," Mother said. "But I think it might be best for now."

"I'll make arrangements in the morning," Simon said.

"Tell your cop friend you're going," I said. "That way, Sullivan will be sure to know."

We left it at that, all of us exhausted. Simon agreed to stay in our guest room, and we all trudged off to bed.

As I drifted off to sleep, I thought about Stella. I'd have to tell her what happened tomorrow when I saw her. With my face bruised as it was, there would be no hiding that I'd been badly beaten.

5

ESTELLE

"What am I supposed to do all day?" I asked Penelope as she put the finishing touches on my hair. "This is ridiculous. Not being able to go out, hiding in here like a mole."

"You have your books," Penelope said.

Charlie, lying at me feet, lifted his head but then seemed to think better of getting involved and plopped his chin over his paws and closed his eyes. "I want to go to work with Mrs. Bancroft like I did before." Before Simon Price ruined everything.

"I know. But for now it's most important that you stay safe."

No sooner had I finished my breakfast than a knock on the front door drew my attention. From my position in the dining room, I heard Penelope walk across the floor to answer the door. Percival had insisted we have a guard during the day as well. Surely he would keep us safe?

Although it was Benny's day off. Had he remembered to inform the other doorman about my situation?

Curious and a little afraid, I went out to see for myself who it was. The sight standing in the foyer, giving his coat and hat to Penelope, weakened my knees and caused my legs to tremble.

My father.

I peeked around him to see the bodyguard. "I'm sorry, Mrs. Wainwright. He said he was your father."

"That's correct. He is."

"Estelle." Father nodded as if he'd only just seen me yesterday.

"What are you doing here? How did you find me?" *And why now instead of when I needed money?*

"May we speak?" He seemed strangely subdued, less bombastic. Certainly, less angry than the last time I'd seen him.

"Yes, come inside. We can talk near the fire where it's warm." I led him into the sitting room. "Penelope, would you please bring us tea?"

"I'd prefer coffee if you have it," Father said. "Your mother and her blasted tea all the livelong day."

"Right away, sir." Penelope hurried away, leaving us alone.

I sat, arranging my skirt to hide my nervousness. "What can I do for you?"

"I've come on behalf of your mother. She wants to know where Mauve and Pierre are living. We have searched for them unsuccessfully."

I twisted my fingers together, preparing to lie. "I don't know. When I left them, Pierre and I agreed it would be better for the baby if I was no longer around. I assumed they were going home to you and Mother." All lies. They had gone to live on Pierre's uncle's vineyard somewhere in the Bordeaux region of France. He'd not told me the exact location or his uncle's last name, but I had the address.

"You've been in the city since then?" Father asked. "Since you gave birth?"

"That's correct. I thought you knew where I was."

"It took a little time, I must admit." He glanced around the opulent room. "Dr. Bancroft treats his mistresses well."

"I'm not his mistress. He's a friend who took pity on me."

He didn't say anything, looking at me with piercing blue eyes. His face had grown jowly, and his skin seemed redder than last I saw him.

"How much do you know about what's happened to me since I left Pierre and Mauve?"

"I know the Bancrofts took you in. Why was unclear. Then we discovered you were no longer there, and I lost you for a time. This is a large city. But Miss Scarlet was kind enough to tell me of your whereabouts."

Right. I should have figured she'd do anything for the likes of my father. He and men like him were her bread and butter, after all.

"Are you aware of the relationship between our two families?" Father asked.

"I am now. I was not aware until recently of what and who you really are." Anger surged, making me brave. "Now I know it all. Including that, you had Dr. Bancroft's father-in-law killed."

"What do you think you know about me?" Father crossed one leg over the other, the fine material of his pants falling right back into place.

"Pierre told me of the nature of your businesses. He also told me you had Constantine killed."

"Why would I do such a thing?" The corners of his mouth twitched, lifting his mustache.

He didn't deny the accusation, only circumvented it with another question.

"I've no idea why you'd do any of the things you've done. But Pierre told me Constantine seemed like a threat to you, and you had him killed. You murdered the man I loved."

"How was I to know you were with child?"

I gaped at him, too shocked to speak for a second or two. "Would that have mattered?"

"Probably not." His gaze moved to Penelope, who brought in a tray of coffee and scones. She put everything on the table that separated Father and me. Although it was mere feet, the gap between us might as well have spanned the Atlantic Ocean from here to France.

"Shall I pour you a cup, sir?" Penelope asked.

"Please. A dash of cream too, if you will," Father said.

How was he so calm? Acting as if he weren't a murderer? I was such a tangle of nerves I wanted to step outside of my own skin for relief.

"Thank you, Penelope," I said after she had fixed Father his coffee.

"Will there be anything else, miss?"

I shook my head. "No, you may go."

We waited until she was out of the room before continuing.

"Let me explain something to you," Father said. "The lifestyle you girls and your mother enjoyed does not come cheap. In life, one must make choices. We cannot have what we want without sacrifice. I'm in the kind of business that requires discretion as well as guts. Some might call it grit. Regardless, I did it all to take care of my family, and the thanks I get are two daughters who have left their mother. She is bereft, thanks to you."

"Thanks to me? You had Connie killed. If you hadn't done that, I would be happily married with a baby. Instead, my life was ruined."

"You ruined your life when you lay with him out of wedlock."

That part was true. I could not deny my culpability in that regard. "I thought we were marrying soon." An image of Connie's hair glistening in the sunshine that afternoon floated across my mind. He'd been beautiful. So good. I'd thought I'd get to watch his hair turn white as we made a life and family together. "You took him from me," I whispered. "I can never forgive you for that."

58

"I didn't come seeking forgiveness. Your mother wants to know where your sister is."

"Are you having someone follow me?" I asked, avoiding the question.

"I promised your mother I'd locate you," he said, avoiding *my* question. "Thus, I had to use whatever methods I could find at my disposal."

"You make it sound as if you don't have goons working for you—doing your dirty work."

"Young lady, you best watch your tongue."

For a moment, I believed him and almost fell into my typical capitulation. However, then I remembered I no longer had to answer to him. I was free. "I won't hold or watch my tongue. Never again. I don't belong to you."

He fixed cold eyes upon me. "This Dr. Bancroft has money, I see. You're obviously well taken care of."

"It's not your concern."

"This arrangement's a common one," Father said without emotion. "For a common whore."

His words stung. Unshed tears scratched my eyelids and closed my throat. After what he did, how could I still care what he thought of me or the name he called me?

"I take it this is a somewhat permanent relationship?" Father asked. "As permanent as this sort of arrangement can be, anyway."

"As I told you, I am not his mistress. He's loyal to his wife."

"Right. Price's daughter. Homicidal, I've heard. No hope for her returning to good health from what I've heard."

"It doesn't matter. Percival's a loyal man. He has a child for whom he wants to set a good example." *Unlike you.*

Taking his cup in hand, he studied me for longer than felt comfortable. I had to keep myself from squirming like a child. "You're in love with him."

"It's not your concern what I feel or don't feel for Dr.

Bancroft. I work for his mother, helping those in need of medical care. In exchange, they've set me up in this apartment."

"Miss Scarlet said you were contemplating working for her." His voice wavered just slightly.

"What do you care?"

"I don't want my daughter lying with men for money," Father said. "Bringing further shame on our family. This is bad enough. I didn't raise you to be a wanton woman."

"Shame? You are a mobster." I elongated each word and put a space between them. "What further shame could be brought than what you've done? How many men have you killed? How many lives have you ruined?"

He raised his voice to just below a full shout. "Everyone respects me. Don't you ever doubt that, you ungrateful little wench."

Not me. I don't respect you.

I was still too afraid of him to say the words out loud, but my God, I felt them in every part of my body and soul.

"Does Mother know the truth of what you did to Connie? Does she know where all the money comes from?"

"Your mother knows better than to question her own husband about such matters. Her job is to look pretty and entertain. Which she has always done well. Fortunately for her. I would have had no trouble ridding myself of her had she ever given me reason to do so."

Ridding himself? What did that mean? Would he have his own wife killed? "Like you did me."

"You left. *You* deserted your mother."

"I couldn't stay and watch my baby being raised by my sister. It was better to leave them be. Surely you can see that."

"In fact, your mother agrees it was the best outcome, given the circumstances. However, it's of no use to either of us because we don't know where Mauve and Pierre are." He slammed his coffee cup back onto its saucer hard enough I thought the china might break. "You will tell me, or you'll be sorry."

"Honestly, Father, I don't know. The day after the baby was born, I gathered my things and headed here to the city. The Bancrofts took me in for a period of time. Until they learned who I really was."

"Yet you're here?"

"Percival took pity on me. He didn't want me to work for Miss Scarlet, so he offered this apartment. As I said." Had I? The longer this conversation went on, the more confused I became. Now that I thought about it, speaking with my father had always been this way.

"The son—Simon Price—he's been making a nuisance of himself. Asking questions he shouldn't be asking. I'll have no choice but to get rid of him if he doesn't shut his mouth and keep to his own affairs."

I cocked my head to the side, examining him. His ruddy complexion was even more obvious since his hair had turned white. He'd grown plump, and bags under his eyes appeared soft and doughy. "Simon figured out who I really am. This was months after I'd come to live here. After the Bancrofts understood you were my father, they asked me to leave. How could I blame them? You destroyed their family."

"I didn't touch the wife. I wouldn't harm a woman," Father said.

"But you do harm them when you kill the men they love. You hurt me when you had Connie killed."

"He did that to himself. I could tell he would cause me trouble. I knew it in my bones."

"So, you had him killed." Not a question.

He shrugged, appearing bored.

"Percival and Simon believe her father's murder helped in Mary's demise," I said. "Their entire family shattered into a thousand pieces because of you."

"It was a business decision," Father said. "Mr. Price disrespected me. He paid for it with his life. I lose no sleep over it."

"What about Connie?" I asked. "Do you lose sleep over killing the man I loved?"

"You seem to have recovered nicely from your broken heart." He smirked.

"What does that mean?"

"You're living here as Percival Bancroft's mistress. I know you well enough to know that it cannot only be about survival. You're too much of a romantic for that to be true."

I stared at him for a moment, shocked by this insight into my character. "My romantic nature was tested and found lacking when I faced hunger and dying on the streets during a cold New York winter."

He grew silent, seemingly contemplating what I'd said. This gave me a small kernel of gratification. "Which led you to Miss Scarlet's doors," he said finally.

"Something like that."

"And this Dr. Bancroft found you there and once again rescued you. Sounds terribly romantic. I suspected he'd seduced you during a vulnerable period in your life, and silly girl that you are, you've fallen in love with him."

"He's not mine to love. He has a wife."

"He's a man of honor, is that it?" Father sneered, his words dripping with sarcasm.

If I had trouble defending myself, I certainly didn't have the same trouble when it came to Percival. Not only did he show me how truly small my father was, he was the best man I knew. Period. No one was better. It was suddenly terribly important that Father understand this. "He is. He truly is. And yes, he rescued me when I was all alone and sick, with nowhere to go. But Percival's not keeping me here to become his mistress but because he's kind and generous. When he found me at Miss Scarlet's, he...he..." What exactly was I trying to say?

"He couldn't bear the idea of other men touching you," Father said. "He wants you to himself. I know men because I am one."

My cheeks flamed, and I could not look at him. "Whether you believe me or not is of no consequence." I managed to raise my gaze to his face.

Father dotted his mouth with a napkin and stood. "I must take my leave. Your mother will be disappointed to hear you do not know of Mauve's whereabouts. Her heart's been broken by you two girls. I never thought I'd see the day. Perhaps you— always headstrong and a little wild—but our sweet little Mauve? No. This is because of Pierre's influence. I should have known better than to let her marry a Frenchman."

Why had he allowed Pierre to live and not Constantine? They both refused to work for him. The difference must be as simple as this: Connie threatened to go to the police, whereas Pierre simply refused a job offer.

"Mauve knows who you are now. Do you really think she would have stayed and let you kill Pierre like you did Connie? Wherever she is, she's safe from you. As far as Mother goes, I'm sorry she's sad, but I can't help—I don't know where Mauve and the baby are. You may tell her I'm alive and well taken care of, therefore she can put me out of her mind if she hasn't done so already." I waited for God to strike me down for my lies, but nothing came. "I'll show you out," I said.

"Very well."

As we entered the foyer, Penelope appeared with his coat and hat.

Father looked at me for a moment, an emotion reflected in his expression I could not decipher. Was it regret? Disappointment? "What you and your sister have done has broken your mother's heart. You might as well both be dead and buried in the ground next to your brother."

63

"Mother should blame the one responsible. We both know who that is."

"You can't prove it was me that killed Constantine." This was said matter-of-factly. A statement by a man who did not have to pay for his actions.

"And therefore it didn't happen?" I asked. "Is that what you tell yourself?"

"You aren't capable of understanding the complexities of my business." Father buttoned the top of his coat. "My father used to tell me that nothing was impossible. There were always solutions to get what we wanted in life. If you want Dr. Bancroft, you're going to have to play dirty."

"I want to be a good person," I said quietly. "That's more important to me than anything else."

"I hope it will be enough to keep you warm at night. Goodbye, Estelle."

I watched as Penelope held the door open for him. The moment he stepped outside to the hallway, she slammed the door behind him.

As hard as I tried to remain stoic, tears flooded my eyes. His indifference hurt. Mother's lack of courage hurt. I was without a family.

"Miss, come rest. You're white as the china."

Penelope clucked sympathetically, then led me back into the sitting room, fussing over me, muttering under her breath about the nerve of some people. Percy would come later tonight for dinner. Although he'd asked for Saturday evenings only, I'd convinced him to come by this evening as well. Thank goodness. I needed to see him.

THE DAY HAD DRAGGED on after Father left, but it was finally time for Percival to arrive. Although it had only been a couple of days since I'd seen him, I ached to be near him. The night before, I'd caught wind through Penelope, who remained friends with the staff at the Bancrofts', that he and his mother were going to a gala at the Ashfords'. I'd attended a ball there during the holidays just two years ago. Strange to think of it now. How different my life had been. Mauve and I had been new debutantes, excited to be included in parties and dances. Both of us romantics, hoping to find true love sooner rather than later. If I'd only known.

Penelope helped me dress with care for my dinner with Percival. The dressmaker had been by earlier with one of my new evening dresses—a blue silk with a dropped waist and lacy collar that flattered my figure.

"You look lovely," Penelope said, standing back from the full-length mirror in my bedroom to look me up and down. "I'd give anything for your thick hair." She touched her fingers to her light blond hair. "Nothing but wisps. I'm too short and round to be fashionable. But I suppose I have my personality, which will last me my whole life, whereas beauty fades."

"You're beautiful inside and out," I said. "If it weren't for you, I'd be terribly lonely."

"Speaking of beauty, I have gossip." Penelope's eyes twinkled. "I think Mr. Foster fancies Mrs. Landry. He came by yesterday to ask her for a recipe. It was quite obvious he likes her."

"Do you think the feelings are returned?"

"It seems so to me."

"How lovely for them. Perhaps we'll have a wedding sometime soon."

I must have sighed because Penelope's expression grew concerned. "What is it?"

"Nothing, really. It's just that I wish...well, never mind. One must get on with things and be grateful for what we have."

"Yes, but sometimes what we want seems bigger than what we have."

I nodded, returning her kind smile in the mirror.

"I shall check with Mrs. Landry about dinner," Penelope said. "And put the final touches on the table. I found the most glorious candlesticks in a drawer."

She left me to take care of her tasks. I wandered into the sitting room, restless and nervous. *Silly*, I told myself. *It's only Percival*. Still, I craved him with a hunger different from an empty stomach. It was a yearning so fierce that I was afraid it might swallow me whole. My father's unwelcome visit had only made me realize with more clarity that the Bancrofts had become my family.

I stood by the fire, warming my hands. Penelope had recently added additional logs, which brightened the room, even though it had grown dark outside hours before.

I felt rather than heard Percival enter through the room. I turned, hummingbirds in my stomach. What in the world? I gasped at the sight of his swollen black-and-blue face.

"My God, what's happened to you?" I asked.

"I'm fine. I'll explain." He took my hands in his, studying me intently. "It's good to see you."

"Were you in an accident?"

"No. Not an accident." He gestured toward the bar. "Let me pour myself a drink, and then we can sit and talk."

"Yes, yes. Whatever you want." Frightened to hear what he would say, I sat in my favorite chair by the fire and pressed my trembling hands together.

He took the chair next to me and tossed back a mouthful of whiskey. "I was attacked last night after I left the Ashfords' party."

My body went numb. I knew before he said it who was responsible.

"It was two of your father's thugs. They asked me, in a manner of speaking, to convince Simon to stop stirring up trouble and to stay away from you."

My stomach felt as if it plunged to the floor. "What do you mean?"

"Simon went to speak to a friend, a cop, about his father's murder. He wants justice. But there's no such thing when it comes to these men. Your father will have Simon killed if he doesn't do as he's told, and there's not a thing any of us can do about it."

"Have you seen Simon? Did he agree?"

"Yes, I spoke to him last night. He's going to leave for Europe as soon as possible."

"That will send a message, no doubt, that he'll leave well enough alone." I twisted my fingers together until my skin whitened. "My father came to see me this morning."

"Here?"

"Yes. He wanted me to tell him where my sister and Pierre are living. They've not been in contact since they left for France."

"Did you tell him?"

"No. I lied to him. I'm ashamed to say it, but I had to." My breath caught, remembering the cruel words he'd said to me. "As much as I despise him, he's still my father, and he still has the power to hurt me. He said a few things—hurtful things."

"What did he say?" Percival growled the words rather than spoke them.

"I can't say it."

"He thinks you're my mistress?"

"Yes. He knows I considered working for Miss Scarlet."

"And he called you terrible names?" Percival asked.

"Correct." I waved a hand in front of my eyes to try to keep the tears from spilling onto my cheeks and ruining Penelope's handiwork with powder and rouge.

"I'm sorry," Percival said. "I'd take it away if I could."

I granted him a smile, even though inside, I felt like crying. "He knows about this arrangement, obviously. I tried to convince him that it was only a friendship we shared, not a romance, but he didn't believe me." Who would? The modern world had become a cynical place. Especially to men like my father.

Echoing my thoughts, Percival said, "Most men wouldn't believe such a thing possible."

"You're not most men." I ached to touch his bruised face but kept my hands folded in my lap instead.

"Did you tell him about Constantine? That you know he had your fiancé killed?" Percival asked.

"I did. He never fully admitted to hiring someone to kill him, but I know it's true. He's good at deflecting. Regardless, I could see the truth in his eyes, even though the man refused to acknowledge that his actions are what ruined his family."

"What now?" Percival asked.

"I don't think he'll return. If Simon's out of the country, Father should leave us alone." I really hoped I was right.

"What about your mother?"

"She doesn't care enough to come see me," I said. "Thus, I mustn't care either."

"But you do."

The compassion in his eyes and the soft, sympathetic curve of his mouth undid me. I covered my face with my hands so that he would not see the ugly way my face contorted when I sobbed.

I felt rather than saw him move from his chair to fall on his knees before me. "I'm sorry for it all," he whispered.

I removed my hands from my damp face to look down at his bent head, close enough I could see the tooth marks made from a comb in his glossy dark hair. "I'll be all right."

He looked up at me. "May I bring Clara to see you tomorrow after church? She might cheer you?"

"All Bancrofts do," I said, smiling through yet another bout of tears.

6

PERCIVAL

As promised, after church Sunday morning, Mother, Clara, and I arrived at Stella's apartment in time for luncheon. The delight on both Clara's and Stella's faces made my eyes sting. They ran to each other, with Stella falling to her knees to enfold my daughter in her arms.

"I've missed you so," Stella said.

"You were gone too long," Clara said before leaning in to whisper something in Stella's ear I could not hear.

"I'm sorry to hear that," Stella said softly, stroking Clara's cheek.

Soon, we were gathered around the dining room table for a first course of split pea soup with bits of ham.

"This is marvelous," Mother said. "Mrs. Landry learned from the best, so I'm not surprised."

We all took another scoop of the warm soup.

"Tell me what you've been doing with yourself since I last saw you," Stella asked Clara.

Clara happily rambled on for a good five minutes about school and her friends and how much she wanted a pony. Stella never took her eyes off my daughter, which warmed my heart.

However, my thoughts drifted this way and that, from Mary to Stella's father to the thugs who'd beaten me up.

I was pulled from my myriad of thoughts when Mother, during a moment when Clara caught her breath, asked me a question about little Maria Rossi. "Is she better?"

I'd gone by to see her before church that morning. "Yes, she's much better." I'd been delighted to see Maria sitting up in bed, with good color in her cheeks. "She'll be back to her usual self in a few days."

"Thank the good Lord," Mother said.

"Who is Maria?" Stella asked.

I explained that she was one of my patients who had been very sick but was now on the mend. "Mrs. Rossi is a widow with too many mouths to feed," I said. "I don't know what their future holds."

This quieted the women around the table. All three of them looked down at their empty soup bowls and let out remarkably similar sighs. They were like three perfect peas sharing the same pod.

The next course arrived, and we went back to eating and chatting about nothing of consequence. That is until Clara said something that made my blood run cold.

"There was a scary man outside of our house today when Grandmama and I went to the park. He followed us all the way there."

"Clara, are you certain?" Mother asked sharply.

"I think so." Clara's voice wavered, obviously frightened by my mother's tone.

"Why didn't you tell me at the time?" Mother asked.

"I don't know. I forgot." Tears glistened in Clara's eyes. "Am I in trouble?"

"No, not in trouble," I said. "But if it ever happens again, please tell one of us."

"All right." Clara nodded solemnly.

I looked across the table at Stella. She'd set aside her fork and was staring down at the plate in front of her.

"Stella?" I asked.

Her chin lifted, and she met my gaze with frightened eyes. I knew without her saying the words that she blamed her father.

"You mustn't go out without an escort," Stella said. "From now on."

"I agree, Mother. You'll take one of the male staff from here on out."

Mother nodded, her lips pursed.

"Do you know what the man looked like?" Stella asked Clara.

"Not his face. His hat was pulled way down, and he had a scarf over his mouth." Clara closed her eyes as if to see him again in her mind. "And he was tall and wide. Bigger than you, Papa."

That didn't give us much to go on, but it didn't really matter. Other than my daughter, we all knew the probable origin of the man who'd followed her. He could be one of the thugs that beat me up or another of Sullivan's men. Regardless, I had no doubt Sullivan had sent whoever he was to spy on my mother and Clara. Had he still been gathering information at that point? He appeared to know everything about us—our routines and habits, including where we lived. None of us were safe. If he wanted us gone, we would be.

"Papa?" Clara asked in a frightened voice. "What's wrong? Is it the same man who hurt you?"

"I don't know." I forced myself to smile. "But it's nothing for you to worry about. Your papa will take care of everything."

If only I could say that with complete confidence. Sean Sullivan was rich, powerful, and ruthless, which made him very dangerous. All of the people I loved were vulnerable.

However, I had to think positively. Simon would be gone soon. All the trouble he'd brought from his inquiries would soon fade. They had to.

BY THE TIME the last day of the year arrived, we'd all earned an evening of relaxation and fun. Stella gave Mrs. Landry and Penelope the night off and agreed to stay at our apartment overnight. I'd have liked to take her and Mother out somewhere, but knew that it would only create curiosity and gossip about our relationship. Instead, Mother asked our cook to make a ham and several other decadent dishes. Stella had asked if Clara could stay up a little later than usual so she could dine with us, and I'd agreed. Our nanny had frowned when I gave her the evening to do as she pleased as if I were trying to pull something over on her.

While I dressed, I sent Joseph to fetch Stella from her place, instructing him to stay alert to any dangers or suspicious activity. They returned without mishap.

I greeted Stella when she came in, looking ravishing in a wine-colored dress that clung to her slender figure. We all gathered in the drawing room for a drink before supper.

"I've been taking piano lessons," Clara said to Stella.

My daughter was dressed for the evening in a blue velvet frock and patent leather shoes. Her dark tresses had been curled and pinned back on the sides. Thrilled to be joining the adults, she sparkled with excitement.

"Do you enjoy them?" Stella asked Clara while taking the glass of sherry I offered.

Clara crinkled her nose. "I don't like to practice all the time, but I do every day because I'm forced to. But I like it a little. Would you like me to play for you?"

"I'd be honored," Stella said, settling into a chair near the fire.

Clara went to the piano in the corner of the room and made a big show of preparing, flexing her fingers and closing her eyes as if waiting for the muse to enter her body. Her hands hovered dramatically over the keys, then she began. She played a few simple tunes that were honestly difficult to recognize. Still, we all clapped politely when she'd finished.

Clara stood from the piano bench and presented us with a deep bow. She might be more suited for the stage than playing an instrument.

"When did you start taking lessons?" Stella asked politely.

"I'm not sure." Clara looked at Mother. "It feels as if it's been forever and a day."

"She started a few months ago." Mother raised both brows. "Definitely not forever and a day."

Robert entered the room, a concerned expression displayed on his usually placid expression. "I'm sorry to interrupt, but there's a phone call for Dr. Bancroft. It's Mrs. Mason from the asylum."

"Mrs. Mason?" It could only be bad news if Mrs. Mason was calling on New Year's Eve. She ran the asylum and called only if absolutely necessary. I exchanged a quick glance with Mother before following Robert into my study.

I picked up the receiver, held it to my ear, and leaned closer to the earpiece. "Hello, this is Dr. Bancroft."

"Doctor, it's Mrs. Mason."

I braced myself. "Yes, how can I help you?"

"I'm sorry to call on a holiday, but I'm afraid this couldn't wait. Your wife's escaped, and we cannot find her on the grounds or anywhere inside the building."

My legs felt as if they might collapse under me. "Did you say escaped?"

"Yes, I'm sorry, Dr. Bancroft."

"How is that possible?" From what I could tell, the place had impenetrable security, both to get in and out.

"We're not certain. Her brother, Simon Price, was here this afternoon. He sat with her in the sunroom for over an hour. After he left, Mary was escorted back to her room for a rest before supper. When one of our attendants stopped in to escort her to the dining hall, she was not in her room. We then did a wide and thorough search and came up empty."

"She couldn't have gotten off the property without help," I said. "Isn't that right?"

"We're unsure, to be perfectly frank. We've questioned the staff, and thus far, no one's confessed to aiding her. As you know, we keep a close watch on all our patients. It's rare they're alone, so we're baffled about how this happened."

Had Simon orchestrated this somehow? But why would he want her to escape? He knew how dangerous and volatile she could be.

"What should I do?" I asked.

"There's not much you can do. The local police have been notified. Volunteers have gathered to conduct a search on foot. I'll keep you informed throughout the night."

She put a member of the local police on the line then, who instructed me to stay home tonight in case she somehow found her way back to her former residence. "You'll want to join the search efforts in the morning, I assume?"

"Yes, I will."

"Hopefully, we'll locate her this evening, but we'll be sure to call with any updates."

By the time I set the receiver back into its holder, my entire body trembled with fear and shock. I ventured back to the sitting room, where Mother and Stella were waiting anxiously to hear why Mrs. Mason would be calling on New Year's Eve. Clara had moved to the table where we played games to work on a puzzle we'd gotten her for Christmas. She looked up at me with inquisitive eyes. "Papa, what's wrong?"

"Nothing, love. But I need to speak to your grandmother about something boring and for adults' ears only." I glanced over at Robert, who stood near the entryway to the room. "Robert's going to take you down to wish the staff a happy new year while they're having their supper."

Clara's cheek flexed the way it did when she really wanted to argue but knew better. "Yes, Papa." She trudged over to Robert.

"Miss Clara, I believe Mrs. Wilson's made a chocolate cake for dessert," Robert said. "Would you like to see it?"

"Yes, please." My daughter's mood drastically altered at the thought of chocolate cake.

Once she was safely out of earshot, I returned my attention to the ladies. I sat next to Mother and drew in a deep breath before speaking. "Mary's escaped the asylum."

Both ladies gasped in unison.

"How is that possible?" Mother asked.

"They're not sure," I said. "Simon was there earlier today. Perhaps his visit prompted some kind of strange response in Mary?"

"He wouldn't help her escape, would he?" Mother asked.

"I don't think so. I'm not sure what his reasoning would be if he did."

Stella hadn't moved for several seconds, her eyes wide with shock. How strange it must be for her. She was part of my family and yet not truly. We could pretend for moments in time that she belonged here with me, but not tonight. Mary's presence was felt as keenly as if she were in the room with us.

Where are you? I asked her silently. *What have you done?*

———

DINNER WAS A MORE somber affair than I'd hoped it would be. Although Mrs. Wilson's meal of roast beef, smashed potatoes slathered in butter, freshly baked rolls, and roasted carrots was impeccable, every bite seemed drier than the last. My stomach churned with nerves and worry, but I kept up a brave face for Clara's sake. Mother and Stella were equally quiet and subdued. Clara, however, didn't seem to sense our moods and she chattered away.

"What was Christmas like when you were a boy?" Clara asked me.

Between Mother and me, we had a lot of memories to share. Happily, this kept the conversation flowing and even distracted me somewhat from thoughts of Mary.

"What about when you were a girl?" Clara asked, directing her attention upon Stella.

"We spent the holidays at our home in the country," Stella said. "It was very cold in the wintertime, and we liked to be outside when we could so that we could skate on our pond. That was our favorite pastime." Her eyes grew wistful. "Even when we were grown, we would skate every afternoon when we were home for school holiday."

"Why does it make you sad to remember?" Clara asked.

"Oh, well…I'm not sad, exactly. It's only that I miss my sister a lot."

"Where is she?" Clara asked.

Stella shot a look in my direction before answering. "She and her husband had to move away."

"How come?" Clara asked.

"Sometimes adults have to make decisions that are hard but for the best," Stella said.

"Like my mother having to go to jail?" Clara asked.

"Not jail, darling," Mother said. "Your mother's sick, remember? She's in an asylum where they help people who have trouble sorting out what's real and what isn't."

Clara blinked but didn't ask anything further. Mother diverted the conversation to our upcoming dessert, which captured Clara's attention nicely.

After our slices of chocolate cake had been devoured, Mother announced it was time for a yawning Clara to go to bed. I expected protests, but she had stayed up several hours past her usual bedtime and was too tired to make a fuss.

"Will you and Stella kiss me good night?" Clara asked as she took my mother's hand.

"Yes, we'll come up in a few minutes," I said.

Once they were gone, I invited Stella to have a drink with me in the sitting room. She agreed with a simple nod of her head.

While Robert poured us each a drink, we sat down in front of the fire. Several new logs had been added, sparking flames that warmed my face.

"Will you be staying up until midnight?" Robert asked as he set our drinks on the table.

"I don't think so," I said. "I'll need to be up early tomorrow morning. Speaking of which, please inform Joseph that I'll need him to take me to the train station at seven. I'm visiting the asylum in the morning."

"Yes sir. Will there be anything else?"

"No, thank you," I said. "Please, you may retire if you wish. I can handle getting myself off to bed."

"Very well, sir."

"What is it?" I asked Stella after he left. "You've barely said a word tonight."

"I'm fine."

"But?" I prompted.

"Do you think my father has something to do with Mary's disappearance?"

I gaped at her for a second or two. The thought had not occurred to me. "Surely not. I mean, what would be his reason for doing so?"

"To scare us?"

"He's done that well enough already, hasn't he?" I asked. "What with having me beaten, you, Mother, and Clara followed? Why would he include Mary in all that? She can't be frightened in the same way we are."

"What if he took her?"

I could see from the panic in her eyes that I could not just simply dismiss her worries. She truly thought it possible. Should I? "Whatever's happened, we'll know soon. If your father had anything to do with this, he will surely bring her back after giving us all a good scare."

"I hope you're right."

"I want you to stay here for the foreseeable future," I said.

"What about Penelope and Mrs. Landry? Do you think they're in danger?"

"No. It's Simon and me he's trying to scare."

"I've done nothing but bring you and your family trouble." Tears glistened in her eyes. "And yet you remain kind and devoted to me. I can't say I understand."

"I've said it before, and I'll say it again. None of this is your fault. Your father's actions are not yours."

Mother appeared in the doorway. Upon inspection, I could see how weary she was. Since Mary's troubles began, life had been hard for me but also for Mother. She'd become a mother to Clara when she should have been enjoying herself as a grand-mother. From my understanding, child-rearing was not nearly the same as being a grandparent. She'd already raised me by herself. She should not have to do it again.

"Clara's ready for you two," Mother said before yawning. "And my darlings, I must beg your forgiveness, but I'll retire as well. The day caught up to me."

"Please, rest, Mother. This has been a long day." I got up to give her a kiss on the cheek. "I'll be leaving early tomorrow morning for the train. I'll call when I know anything."

"Thank you." She turned to Stella. "My maid has your room prepared. I'll see you in the morning for a late breakfast? Around nine?"

"Lovely. Thank you."

The three of us climbed the stairs but parted ways so that Stella and I could go to Clara's room. Expecting her to be awake and looking at a picture book, I was surprised to see that she'd fallen asleep while waiting for us.

I kissed her forehead and adjusted the blankets. "Good night, precious one."

Stella peered down at the sleeping form of my daughter. "Isn't she adorable?"

I smiled. "Indeed."

Once we were back in the hallway, I bade her good night. "Please, try to get some sleep. It's been a tiresome evening."

"You as well."

We stood for a moment, looking into each other's eyes, so much unsaid between us, before heading to our rooms. The moment I walked away from her, I missed her. At least I knew she was safe for the time being, anyway.

As I undressed for bed, I thought back on the evening. When Clara was grown, would she recall the last day of 1922? Would she have fond memories? Or would the cloud of her mother's terrible illness ruin the evening as it as it had mine? This was my life. Not a thing I could do to change it. I had promised Mary Price to care for her in sickness and in health. If only I had hope that she would regain her health. At this point, I knew it was very unlikely.

And I'd moved on with things. I'd not meant to, but I could not lie to myself. I wanted Stella. I wanted her tonight and forever. Although the love for Mary remained, she was not the woman I'd married. Or thought I'd married, anyway. Was it so wrong that a lonely man had fallen in love with another when his wife had virtually disappeared?

Regardless, I'd taken vows before God. To break them was a sin. Admitting my feelings to myself filled me with shame, but it seemed I was powerless to resist them.

I went to bed with the sick feeling of guilt, my only companion. Mary was missing, and here I was pining for another woman. Perhaps I was a monster.

7

ESTELLE

During the last hours of 1922, I tossed and turned, unable to fall asleep. Although Percival had tried to reassure me my father had nothing to do with Mary's disappearance, I was not at all certain he was correct. There were too many connections between my family and the Prices for me to feel confident that this latest incident was unrelated.

I just couldn't figure out why. Why would my father want to harm Mary? She was innocuous, locked away in an asylum, and not mentally capable of hurting my father in any way. On the other hand, Simon had snooped around and visited the police—it made sense that this would have worried Father. He didn't want to go to jail for murder or for the dozen other crimes he'd most likely committed. Keeping Simon quiet made sense. Abducting Mary? Not at all.

But then again, maybe I was incorrect. It could be that Mary got confused and wandered outside. Or she might be hiding somewhere in the building, scared and delusional.

What had transpired during Simon's last visit to her? Had he told her he was leaving for an indefinite amount of time? If so, had that caused her to become sufficiently agitated enough to run away?

Finally, around two in the morning, I fell asleep, waking around six to the sound of footsteps in the hallway. Percival readying himself for his trip to the asylum. I yearned to accompany him and support him in what would be a horrific day. However, I knew it was not my place to go.

Instead, I decided to go home. Confronting my father, asking him for the truth, was the only path I could take. I would be brave and firm. He would give me answers, one way or the other.

AFTER I'D BATHED and dressed, I went downstairs to speak with Mrs. Bancroft. I found her in the dining room, drinking a cup of coffee and reading the newspaper. As always, breakfast was laid out on the buffet.

"Good morning, dear," Mrs. Bancroft said. "You look tired. Were you unable to sleep? I had a terrible night myself."

"Not much, I'm sorry to say." I poured myself a coffee and placed a roll and a dab of scrambled eggs onto my plate. "I can't stop thinking my father has something to do with this."

She looked at me sharply. "I have other theories."

"Meaning Simon?"

"Perhaps. But then again, why?"

"I want to go see my father today," I said. "Confront him face-to-face."

"Wasn't the visit the other day enough? Do you really need more abuse?"

"I need to look him in the eye and ask him if he did something to Mary. I'll know. I have to know. I can be there within hours if I take the train."

"And if he did have something to do with her disappearance?"

"I haven't gotten that far," I said.

"Fair enough." She splayed her hands on the table. "I'll go with you. We'll have Joseph take us to the train station the minute he's back home from dropping Percy."

The idea of Mrs. Bancroft meeting my parents made me feel lightheaded. What would she think of me then? "I won't be welcome, thus, it may be ugly. I've no idea how my mother will react."

"I'll be there with you. If that will make it easier?"

"It will, yes."

"Then that's what we'll do."

ON THE MOSTLY EMPTY TRAIN, Mrs. Bancroft and I sat quietly, both of us pensive. I kept my eyes on the scenery outside the window, pressing rising panic inward. My stomach churned as we headed north, past the dense urban environment with rows of apartment buildings, warehouses, and factories. Automobiles and horse-drawn carriages rambled along busy streets. We crossed the Harlem River, which was filled this morning with boats. The scenery transitioned into residential areas as we traveled through the Bronx and Yonkers. Small houses, parks, and suburban streets presented a quieter life than the one we'd left in the city.

Soon, the landscape shifted to more open spaces, with occasional glimpses of golf courses and small towns.

As we entered Connecticut, the train passed through the affluent suburban towns of Greenwich and Stamford where the sight of large estates, manicured lawns, and tree-lined streets should have calmed my nerves but instead elevated them. The palms of my hands and the nape of my neck dampened with perspiration, despite the chill of the afternoon.

"Do you think about the baby?" Mrs. Bancroft asked me.

For a second, I didn't answer, surprised by the question.

"You don't have to talk about it," Mrs. Bancroft said. "I'm curious, that's all."

"I thought the pain would fade, but it hasn't. There's not an hour in the day that I don't wonder how she is or what she's doing. I did the right thing. That gives me comfort."

Mrs. Bancroft looked out the window, longing etched across her pretty features. "Perhaps someday you will have another child."

"It's unlikely. I've had to accept that."

"If only Percival…well, never mind," Mrs. Bancroft said. "You know what I think."

I squeezed her gloved hand with my own. "I do know."

We quieted as the landscape turned rural, with rolling hills, forests, and farmland. Occasionally, I spotted a farmhouse or a barn, as well as fields with crops and livestock.

We arrived at the Litchfield depot before noon. The station bustled with travelers and goods. Were any of them headed toward a destination that made them feel as if cement had baked into the soles of their shoes, making each step harder than the next?

"Courage, love," Mrs. Bancroft said. "I am here." She left me to speak with the attendant in the ticket box, and soon, a young man named Jack arrived, offering to take us up to my father's estate in his motorcar.

"You're headed to the Sullivans'?" Jack asked, touching the rim of his newsboy-style cap. "Do they know you're coming? I heard they're none too friendly to strangers."

"I'm Estelle Sullivan," I said. "Sean Sullivan's my father."

"Ah, yes." Jack's cheeks flushed but he smiled politely. "I thought I recognized you. Have you been away?"

"I live in New York City now," I said. "So, yes."

A flicker of recognition sparked in his eyes. He'd suddenly remembered the story of my dead fiancé. Word traveled fast here in the quiet countryside. "I'm sure your family will be happy to see you," Jack said. "I know my parents always are, and I live just down the road from them."

If only it were as simple as that.

Mrs. Bancroft and I dipped our heads to crawl into the back seat of the motorcar. Jack drove us down the dirt road toward home.

Hoarfrost covered every branch, shrub, and blades of dead winter grass, creating a crystalline coating that lent the landscape a sparkling, otherworldly appearance. Mauve had always marveled at mornings such as these, thinking them magical. I ached with missing her. How could I have known how losing her felt like the loss of a limb or major organ? I imagined her holding Mireille, bouncing her on her lap, covering her cheeks with kisses. Mauve was the embodiment of love. I should know. I'd been the recipient all my life.

"It's a winter wonderland," Mrs. Bancroft said.

Surprised to see it so icy this late in the morning, I asked Jack about the weather.

"Yeah, the temperature dropped to well below zero overnight," Jack said. "And without sun or rising temperatures, nothing's melted."

Mrs. Bancroft and I exchanged a look. If it were this cold here, then the area around the asylum would be, too, as it was not far from here. If Mary had somehow gotten outside overnight, she would not have survived. Not in this weather.

A hollow, horrible feeling made me feel almost dizzy. What would Percival face today? He'd had so much pain in his life, and I feared more was coming. If she were dead, he would be overwhelmed with guilt and remorse. Would it debilitate him for years to come?

I couldn't think about the future. Not today. I owed it to Percival to do what I could to discover the truth. That was the only way to help him.

We were now at the wrought iron gate, with its swirling scrollwork and delicate filigree. Our family monogram crafted in gold leaf adorned the center of the gate's doors. Tall, robust stone pillars with lions' heads placed atop stood on each side.

I took it all in with eyes that had been reborn during my absence. The opulence of the metal gate and lion marble statues had seemed ordinary to me, but I now saw them anew. I was not the same woman who had left in shame. I was now a survivor, a fighter.

As was typical this time of day, the gate had been left open for deliveries and the comings and goings of staff. Jack drove down the meticulously maintained gravel driveway lined with trimmed hedges and stately trees that curved gracefully toward the mansion.

Made of finely cut limestone, with a series of grand arched windows, each framed with ornate stone carvings and topped with decorative keystones, my father's home was indeed a sight to behold. At the center of the facade, a magnificent portico extended outward, supported by a row of Corinthian columns carved with acanthus leaves and fluted shafts. Above the portico, a balustraded balcony provided a vantage point over-looking the manicured front gardens. My father had often stood there, looking out upon his estate like a benevolent leader of a small country.

My gaze traveled up to the roofline of the mansion, adorned with a series of dormer windows, each with its own decorative gable and trim. Ornate cornices ran along the edge of the roof, and stone quoins accentuated the corners.

"I never saw it this close-up," Jack said under his breath.

"Stunning," Mrs. Bancroft said in a tone that belied the compliment.

Until this past year, I'd not thought much about my family's wealth. I'd not known where it came from or how easy it had made my life. Yet none of this had ever been mine. Not really. This was my father's world.

We stepped from the car, gravel crunching beneath our feet. Today, the manicured lawns, dormant flower beds, and carefully pruned topiaries were covered in the same hoarfrost we'd seen on the way.

I needed only to close my eyes to see the back gardens with the lush foliage, fountains, and winding pathways. A reflecting pool, our private tennis court, and a stable for horses that had been available to Mauve and me every day of our lives. How I'd taken them for granted. There was our secret garden, too, where we'd spent so many hours together playing among the flowers and trees.

And Robbie. Before we'd lost him, how we'd fussed over and petted our cherubic baby brother. He was the first of a series of losses. All of which seemed to have defined my life. How could I hold so much loss in one body? And heart.

I took Mrs. Bancroft's arm as we climbed up the wide stone staircase to the mahogany front door. Upon our arrival, I glanced at her for courage. She gave me a slight nod. "You'll be fine."

The door was answered by the butler, James, who had been with my family for years. His eyes widened in surprise to see me standing there before his usually stoic expression shifted into a warm smile. "Miss Estelle. How good to see you."

"Thank you, James. I'm here to call on my mother and father. Are they available?"

"Come in from the cold." He gestured for us to step inside. "While I inquire."

We stepped through the grand mahogany door, and the opulence of my childhood home enveloped me. The polished marble floors and the grand staircase that swept upward felt strange as if they belonged to someone else's family instead of my own. The scent of beeswax polish filled the air, mingling with the faint aroma of woodsmoke from distant fireplaces. The high ceilings adorned with ornate plasterwork and crystal chandeliers should have cast a warm, inviting glow, but instead, the light seemed harsh and cold.

"Please wait here. I won't be a moment." James hurried off, his heeled shoes clicking on the marble floor.

Mrs. Bancroft's eyes, sharp and discerning, appeared to take in every detail with a mix of admiration and scrutiny. "It's certainly grand," she murmured.

"Indeed."

James reappeared, asking us to follow him to the library. "Your mother will be right down and asked if you would care for refreshment."

"That won't be necessary," I said. "How did she seem? Mother?"

"I can't say exactly. Surprised?" James asked.

The moment we entered the library, the rich aroma of leather-bound books and polished wood greeted me as familiar as an old friend. Had James brought me here because he knew it was my favorite room in the house? Perhaps he'd remembered that this had been a quiet refuge and a place to lose myself in the pages of countless stories. As a child, I'd felt invisible most of the time. Mauve's shine had been so bright that I'd melted away in the glare. Yet maybe someone had noticed me. Even if only because he was paid to do so.

I took it all in for a moment. The tall mahogany bookshelves lined the walls from floor to ceiling, their shelves bowing slightly under the weight of countless volumes. Soft amber light from brass sconces cast a warm glow. An ornate Persian rug, its intricate patterns and rich colors softened by years of footsteps, covered the polished hardwood floor. How often Mauve and I had frolicked there as children, making up games or playing with our marbles or dolls.

My gaze moved to the comfortable leather armchairs, their cushions worn and softened by years of use, each accompanied by a small side table, perfect for resting a cup of tea or a stack of books. As we'd grown older, we'd slowly given up our childhood games in favor of reading. I'd known even then what a privilege it was to have so many books at our disposal.

Had I known the true nature of my father's business, would it have made any difference in my enjoyment? If I'd imagined he would have the man I loved killed, would I have run away screaming? The questions that plagued me now could never be answered. Now that I understood the true nature of my father, everything had changed.

A large, intricately carved desk stood in one corner of the room, its surface cluttered with inkwells, quills, and a collection of neatly stacked papers. A green banker's lamp cast a pool of soft light over the desk, its glow reflecting off the polished wood and the brass fittings.

Mauve and I had sat there together in the afternoons doing homework, content to be together, despite the strangeness of our mother.

Nothing had changed, it seemed, except for me.

"Did you study here at the desk?" Mrs. Bancroft asked.

"Yes, often." I smiled, remembering those happy afternoons. "My sister too. We'd pull two chairs up to the desk and study as if we were one person."

A rolling ladder attached to a brass rail allowed access to the highest shelves. The windows, draped with heavy velvet curtains, let in slivers of light that danced across the room, highlighting the dust motes that floated lazily in the air. In one corner, a small fireplace crackled softly.

Mrs. Bancroft moved toward one of the armchairs and sat down. "I can imagine this was your favorite place in the house," she said softly, her eyes scanning the rows of books with appreciation.

"It was. Losing myself in books were some of the happiest times of my life. It was safe inside a book."

"Yes, isn't it the grandest way to spend your time?" Mrs. Bancroft asked.

While we waited, I ran my fingers along the spines of the books, feeling the texture of the leather and the raised gold lettering that hinted at the treasures within.

A few minutes later, Mother arrived, wearing a modest day dress that matched her blue eyes. She stood near the entryway, staring at me as if I were a ghost from the past. I supposed I was.

Mother glided over to me—mere walking was for peasants. However, as elegant as she was, there was something wrong. She'd always had an air of fragility, mostly to do with her slender build and fair skin, yet today, it appeared heightened. She'd grown thinner, and her face seemed drawn and tight. Her eyes, which had at times sparkled in a similar fashion to Mauve's, seemed to have permanently dimmed.

"Good afternoon, Mother." I drew in a breath, trying not to cry. As complicated as my feelings were—and goodness, they were complex—she was still my mother, and I loved her. Regardless of the past, I craved her love and approval, even though I knew I would never get them. Was there anything sadder than knowing one's own mother has abandoned you?

"Hello, Estelle," Mother said, then glanced at Mrs. Bancroft, who had stood to greet her hostess.

"This is my friend, Mrs. Bancroft," I said. "She kindly agreed to keep me company today."

"It's a pleasure," Mother said, holding out her hand. No matter what, her manners were impeccable.

"The pleasure's mine," Mrs. Bancroft said. "Forgive our intrusion upon your afternoon."

"Not at all. What may I do for you?" Mother turned back to

me, speaking casually, as if I merely lived down the road and frequently visited. So much so that if Mrs. Bancroft hadn't known the truth, she might have thought there was nothing hurtful between us.

"I came to talk to Father," I said.

Before Mother could answer, a maid came in with a tray of tea and pastries. After she'd poured, Mother dismissed her and turned to me. "What is it you want with your father?"

I stiffened at the cold tone of her voice. "It's rather complex," I said tightly.

"Well, I'm afraid it's impossible. He's out. In fact, he rarely comes home. He has an apartment in the city. Of late, he prefers to stay there." Mother plucked at an imaginary crumb from her skirt. "He liked for us to be out here in the fresh air, but much of his work is conducted in the city."

Work? She said it with reverence, as if criminal activity were a vocation.

"He came by to see me the other day," I said.

"I'm aware." Mother folded her hands in her lap and let out a long, martyred sigh. "However, he came back to me with no more information than when he left."

My stomach churned at her pious tone. She would never forgive me for having a child out of wedlock. That was as clear as the row of bookshelves behind her. It was as if I'd never been part of this family. I drew in a deep breath before speaking the lie that had become so familiar. "Mother, I don't know where Mauve is. Truly. Otherwise, I would have written to her. I'd like to know how they're doing as much as you. You're not the only one missing a daughter."

That seemed to take the breath out of her. She clutched the collar of her dress. "Before they disappeared, Mauve wrote to me. She told me the baby was a girl and what she'd named her. That was all."

"I'm sorry," I said. "But for a variety of reasons, she thought it best they go away."

"It must have been terribly painful to let go," Mother said. "Of your sister and Mireille."

Was that a hint of sympathy in her voice?

"It was. Regardless, I knew it was better if Mauve and Pierre raised her. It was an act of sacrifice for my baby's sake. I may not get to be her mother, but I can act as if I am."

Mother nodded. "It was a brave thing to do. You were right. If only Mauve could find a way to forgive your father, we could be together again."

"Without me, that is." I looked her directly in the eyes.

"No one sent you away, you know," Mother said. "You chose to do so."

"Mother, that's a lie. Father said I was no longer welcome. Even if he hadn't, Father made sure of that when he had Connie killed. How could I possibly live under the same roof with a man who murdered the man I loved? His selfish, ruthless act ruined my life."

"You sound like a lunatic," Mother said. "Or, at the very least, like a woman with a very active imagination."

"I'm not mad," I said without emotion, even though the pain was so intense I could barely breathe. "I'd just like you to admit the truth about what went on in this house."

I glanced at Mrs. Bancroft, who sat quietly, with one eyebrow raised imperviously and her shoulders squared as if poised for an attack, like a mama bear protecting her cub. Only she wasn't my mother. My mother had paled and stared down at her hands. She would not protect me. She never had.

For a split second, an image played before my eyes. It was a day or two after Robbie's death, and the nanny had sent me outside to play, as I had been acting like a caged animal all morning. Mauve, on the other hand, had sat quietly in her mourning dress, discreet tears gathering at the corners of her eyes but without drawing attention to herself. In fact, she'd barely said a word since we'd been told of Robbie's death. Glad to be free of the stuffy house that now smelled of death and lilies, I'd run out to what Mauve and I called our secret garden.

I'd curled into a ball between two trees, not caring about the dirt or bugs or anything but feeling close to the spot where I'd recently played with my precious little brother. With my cheek pressed into the dirt, sobs had racked my body until I'd worn myself out. I'd gone inside, suddenly yearning for Mauve. Our nanny had taken one look at me and sent me upstairs to wash up and change my dress.

As I'd walked down the hallway to our nursery, I passed Mother's room, knowing I was not welcome. However, the sound of an animal howling in pain had stopped me in my tracks. My heart had pounded in my chest, and my pulse seemed to beat from the pit of my stomach in throbbing spasms. It was not an animal but rather my mother, crying for her baby boy. A primal sound that came from the very essence of her grief—it had frightened me more than anything ever had. To hear one's mother in that kind of agony shakes one to the core. It was as if I were on a swaying ship with nothing to hold on to.

All of this ran through my mind in the moments before Mother surprised me by lifting her gaze toward Mrs. Bancroft. "Mrs. Bancroft, would it be possible for you to give me a few minutes alone with my daughter?"

"Is that all right with you?" Mrs. Bancroft asked me.

I nodded in agreement, as my mouth was too dry to speak. Mother called for James and asked that he escort Mrs. Bancroft to the sitting room.

"I shall wait patiently. Please, take your time," Mrs. Bancroft said kindly before following the butler out of the room.

Once she was gone, I expected Mother to say whatever it was she wanted to say to me, but she didn't. She merely gazed blankly into the fire.

"How much do you know about Father's work?" Perhaps she had been in the dark as Mauve, and I had been?

"I know enough to know how blessed we are with material wealth. Anyway, it's not a woman's place to question her husband's business. My job is to take care of his children and his home."

Take care of his children?

I'd had enough. My temper flared out of my belly, unleashing words I never would have thought I'd have the courage to say. "Mother, how can you live this way? Knowing he's the one who caused all of this to happen? You simply look away, letting him take everyone you love?"

She looked me straight in the eyes. "I have no idea what you're talking about."

I studied her with more intent than I'd ever done anything in my life. Was she speaking the truth? She'd not known?

"Tell me," Mother said. "Tell me what you think he's done."

"He approached Connie before the wedding and told him about his business and that he would expect Connie to work for him. I don't know the details of the interaction because, on his way to talk to me, he was killed. It wasn't an accident, Mother. Father had Connie killed. I'm assuming Connie refused the job offer, such as it was, and perhaps even threatened to go to the police. Because of that, Father had my fiancé killed."

Mother didn't speak or move for at least a minute. During a second of madness, I thought she might have fallen asleep with her eyes open.

"How do you know this to be true?" Mother lifted her gaze to me, her eyes appearing more flinty gray than blue. "Is it speculation, or do you have proof?"

"Pierre told me everything he knew, which added up to an unbearable truth. It's the reason he took Mauve and Mireille away."

"Because of this supposed thing your father did?"

Annoyed at what appeared to be purposeful obtuseness, I almost snapped at her, but then I realized she was genuine. She'd been here all these months with no communication from either of her daughters. For the first time in a long time, I was filled with pity for her. She'd lost everything because of Father. Surely she could see this? "Pierre didn't think he could keep his family safe if they continued to live here. How could he really, when he knew that Father had ordered the hit on Connie?"

"This cannot be," Mother whispered. "Surely this cannot be."

"You didn't know?" I hated to admit to myself how desperately I hoped she hadn't known. At least then, I could tell myself that she loved me. She'd been kept in the dark, that's all.

"There is much about your father's life and work I'm not privy to," Mother said, lifting her chin. "And I can tell you—this horrible thing he did—I did not know. But I understand now. You and Mauve worked it out between you without any thought to my feelings."

"You could have earned the right to be part of our lives, but you refused," I said quietly.

"How did I refuse?"

"By going along with him. By pushing the truth to the side in exchange for all of this." I waved my hand around to indicate the mansion in which she currently resided. "If Father hadn't ordered Connie's murder, we would all still be here. I'd be married, raising our child."

"I see now. I do." Mother pulled her hankie from her sleeve and brought it to her face. "I'd not thought him capable of taking Constantine from you."

"Why did he put money ahead of me? Of us?"

"I can't say I understand him, but these are dangerous men he runs with. Clearly, he felt he had no choice but to protect himself."

"How much have you known?" I asked.

"He keeps it away from me. Just as he did you girls."

"Maybe I saw only what I wanted to see," I said. "I've been thinking about that since I found out who he really is."

"You know as well as I that, as women, we have little power over anything in our lives. First, we answer to our fathers. Then to our husbands. Sean made sure I knew it was not my place to ask questions."

"It's the easier path for everyone, it seems," I said.

"Do you think he would have had Pierre killed?" Mother asked.

"I don't know. But Pierre thought it was enough of a possibility that he left, with no plans to return."

Mother's face crumpled, and she began to cry into her hankie. "I've lost you all, haven't I?"

"I didn't think you cared about me or even Mauve. Only Robbie."

She stared at me through watery eyes. "Is that what you thought? Truly?"

"You left us after he died. Not physically, but in here." I patted the side of my head. "You were a ghost in this house." We'd been raised by nannies and the house staff. I didn't say that out loud, afraid to hurt her further. As angry and bruised as I was, my instinct to take care of Mother was stronger.

"Yes, I suppose I was. The grief overpowered me—stripped me of motherly instincts. What you say is true, and I'm sorry. I'm not strong like you, Estelle. Or your sister. Life has proven too much for me."

I had no idea what to say. Again, the echo of her howls played between my ears.

"When Robbie died, we all changed," I said finally. "Mauve and I adored him too."

"I remember." A ghost of a smile appeared, but only for a second. "Why did you come here today?"

"I need to talk to Father."

"Have you changed your mind about telling him where

95

Mauve and Pierre are living?" A flicker of hope sparkled in her reddened eyes.

"Oh, Mother. I'm sorry, but I'm telling you God's honest truth. I don't know where they are." Still no lightning strike from the Lord above. It had to be this way. God help me.

"Then what do you want with your father?"

I hesitated, closing my eyes as I gathered my thoughts. How much to tell her? That was the question. It would be easier to just walk away. Leave all of this behind. Thank her for her time and depart to my new life. But then I remembered the expression on Percival's face when he got the news of Mary's disappearance. I had to do this for him. He needed to know what had happened to his wife.

"It's complicated, but I'll try to explain. Percival's wife lost her mind after the birth of her daughter, and he had no choice but to admit her to an asylum. She was dangerous to the baby and Percival, as well as herself. But right before that, Father ordered the death of Percival's father-in-law. He had Mary Bancroft's father killed over some kind of business dispute."

I went on to tell her about how I'd met Percival that awful day on the train. "I was sick with complications from birth, and he and his mother took me in," I told her the rest of the story, including how they'd asked me to leave once they discovered my true identity. I left out the part about the brothel but described how Percival had changed his mind and offered to take care of me.

"Your father told me of your arrangement. I'm assuming you're his mistress?" Mother asked.

"No, I'm not that. I told Father that when he came to see me, but he obviously doesn't believe me. Percival and I are friends. That's all. Even though no one seems to think so, it's the truth. Percival's a man of great principle and faith. He would never offer the kind of arrangement you speak of. He simply doesn't have it in him."

"How unusual. Men do not often display such honor."

"I suppose they don't." I thought of Mrs. Bancroft's late husband. He'd died in the arms of his mistress. Father clearly had liaisons of his own that Mother seemed to accept as part of marriage. Percival would not be that kind of man, even if it meant depriving himself of someone he truly wanted.

I explained my work at Mrs. Bancroft's side and the time I spent with Clara. "I hope this repays them a little for their kindness, but mostly, they've kept me from...giving up. Percival, well, he's simply the finest man I've ever known."

"You're in love with him," Mother said. "Don't bother saying you aren't because, despite my terrible failings as a mother, I know you. But surely you see that this is doomed."

It was as if someone suddenly punched me in the chest. I lost my ability to breathe for a few seconds. My mother knew me. "Believe me, I understand that. Mary Bancroft's very much alive. Or, at least, we think she is. She disappeared last night. No matter what I want for myself, I could never wish anyone death."

"Isn't it strange what good people you and Mauve are?" Mother asked, sounding wistful and contemplative at the same time. "Despite your parents? You're able to stay dedicated to your values, even though you desperately want him."

Another moment of muteness overtook me. I'd not thought my mother ever paid enough attention to me to understand me at all, let alone to this depth. "It doesn't matter what I feel or not, he's not mine to love."

"My poor girl."

"Do you know the first thing I thought of when Percival received the telephone call last night? That Father had something to do with it."

Mother's color vanished from her cheeks. "Why would he do such a thing?"

"I don't know. I hope I'm wrong. But they were rivals who fought over distribution territories. Did you know that?"

"I'm not involved in your father's business, but yes, I was aware of their...relationship."

"I can't imagine why he would want to hurt the daughter, especially if she's so unwell, but it seems too coincidental."

"Don't speak to him about any of this," Mother said. "Please. Asking him questions will only cause us more trouble."

I nodded, knowing that unleashing more of his rage would not be easy on anyone. Maybe most of all, my mother.

"Anyway, you don't know what's happened yet," Mother said. "Perhaps she's only lost? If your father was involved, no one will ever uncover the truth. He has ways of making sure."

"Mother, are you all right? Does he...hurt you?"

"No, no, nothing like that. I mean, he would never hit me or do bodily harm. His punishment is more of the silent variety. Since he's been in the city, I've had some peace. Or loneliness, depending on how you look at it."

"I'm sorry," I said. "I understand what it's like to be lonely."

"It breaks my heart to see what's happened to our family. I wanted only for you and Mauve to have good lives with good men. Not marriages like mine. But it's not wise to wish or even pray for such a thing. Not when you're married to Sean Sullivan." Her eyes grew glassy and unfocused. "Do you think they're safe? Wherever they are?"

"Pierre promised me he'd take care of them, and he will."

She reached over to take my hand briefly before returning it to her own lap. "I know what it's like to lose a child. It's the worst pain in the world."

"Yes, it is." I started to cry.

"I wish it had all been different for you. But maybe you'll have your chance with Percival. A new baby. A fresh start."

"Mother, there's nothing in the world I'd like more, but it's not meant to be. He's a married man."

"Yes, of course. But I'm your mother, and I'd like to remain hopeful that you will have a happy ending. I'm afraid I must rest now." Mother rose to her feet and stared down at me with the saddest eyes I'd ever seen. "Despite everything, it was very good to see you."

I stood, and she took both my hands in hers, peering at me as if she searched my very soul. "Please know how proud I am of you for making such a hard decision to leave Mireille. You're going to have a good life. Soon, everything will fall into place. I know it will." She pulled me into an embrace. I was much taller than her, but her arms felt strong and tight around me. I drew in the scent of her rosewater cologne. "I've not said it enough, my dearest, but I love you. Don't forget that. No matter what happens."

"I love you too," I whispered, fighting yet more tears.

Mother gave me one last weak smile and left, her shoes click-clacking down the hallway until there was no sound in the room but the crackling of the fire and my rapid breath.

Soon, Mrs. Bancroft appeared in the doorway. At the sight of her, I burst into tears. She took me in her arms, and I wept into the fabric of her dress until it was as damp as my eyes. When I'd gotten control of myself, I pulled away, dabbing at my face with a hankie.

"Darling girl, shall we go home?" Mrs. Bancroft asked. "Clara will cheer us, I'm sure."

I only nodded, following her meekly out of the room. James offered to have one of the men drive us back to the train station. Grateful for the help, we agreed.

As I stepped out of the front door, like a visitor instead of a family member, I wondered if it would be the last time I did so.

8

PERCIVAL

I'd arrived at the asylum without mishap by midmorning. I
was shown to Mrs. Mason's office and waited for a few
minutes before she showed up, looking harried and
distressed. Normally, she was neatly dressed and coiffed, but
today, she had the appearance of a woman who had not slept
much the night before. Her silver hair, although pulled back
into a bun, had come partly undone, and her dress was wrinkled, looking as if she'd slept in it. Maybe she had, I thought,
noting the sofa near the window of her office. As wretched as I
felt over the situation, I couldn't help but pity her.

She plopped into the chair behind her desk. "Dr. Bancroft, I
can't begin to tell you how sorry I am."

"Please, tell me everything you know." Her apologies,
although appreciated, were not going to help us find my wife.

"Yes, of course." She went on to describe the events that led
up to her disappearance and what had been done thus far to
find her. None of it was much different from what she'd told me
over the phone. However, hours and hours had passed since
that conversation, including nightfall and frigid temperatures.
She'd been gone all night. If she'd wandered into the woods and

gotten lost, there was little hope of finding her alive. But wouldn't I know if she was gone? Wouldn't I feel it if the mother of my beloved child had passed away?

"For now, the local police and the volunteers continue to look for her," Mrs. Mason said.

"I shall join them," I said.

"The police chief would like to speak with you first. He said to let him know when you arrived. Thus far, he and his deputies have interviewed every staff member. They're now working on some of the patients to see if anyone remembers anything. But these poor souls rarely say anything sensible, so I doubt they'll get much out of them."

A knock on her office door drew our attention. It was one of the secretaries asking if Chief Wallace could enter.

Mrs. Mason gave her consent as she rose to her feet. "Yes, please show him in."

Chief Wallace was a rotund, ruddy-cheeked man with an unlit tobacco pipe dangling from the corner of his mouth. We exchanged pleasantries before Mrs. Mason excused herself. "I'll just be down the hall if either of you need anything."

"I'm sorry to have to put you through all this," Wallace said. "It's my understanding your wife's been here six years?"

"Give or take," I said.

"Mrs. Mason gave me details about why she's here, so I'll spare you having to go through it all with me. However, I do need to understand your whereabouts the last several days."

My stomach fluttered with nerves. "Sure, what do you need to know specifically?" It hadn't occurred to me until just this moment that I could be a suspect.

What ensued were questions about where I'd been during the time of her disappearance, which I answered as best I could. It wasn't hard to remember, since it was only yesterday. I described our activities, including celebrating the new year with Mother, Clara, and Stella.

"Who is Stella?" Wallace asked, his small eyes growing even smaller as he peered at me from over a pair of round glasses that sat on the end of his nose.

This is where I hesitated, unsure how to answer. Who was Stella, after all? Who was she to me, for that matter? If I told him who and what she was to me, would that make me look even more suspicious?

"Stella Wainwright is a friend of mine and my mother's," I said after a few too many seconds had passed.

"A friend? I see." He dropped his gaze to scribble something in his notebook.

"She works with my mother." Darn, my voice. Why was it wobbling as though I was guilty?

"What kind of work is that?" Wallace's mustache quivered.

"They help to look after some of my poorer patients. There are whole neighborhoods without medical care."

"Is this the same woman you…how shall I say it? Pay for her apartment and life because she's your mistress?"

"She's not my mistress. As I said, she's a good friend of our family, that's all."

"Well, it would give you motive for killing your wife if you were to have, let's say, fallen in love with another woman?"

"It would, yes. But it didn't." I looked him straight in the eyes, hoping he would see the truth in mine. "I've been loyal to my wife all these long years. As hard and lonely as it's been, I made a vow before God and have no intention of breaking it."

"I see. How noble of you."

I didn't know what he wanted me to say or do to defend myself, so I said nothing.

"Do you think they'll find your wife alive?" Wallace asked.

My mouth opened and closed like a fish out of water. "I have no idea. I can tell you I'm concerned. The weather's been below-freezing for nights in a row. If she was out in it last night, I don't know how she would have survived."

He asked a few more questions, and I answered woodenly. The longer he was with me, the further away he got from discovering what had actually happened.

"Do you agree it would be easy to murder her, given that all that would take is leading her into the forest and leaving her there to freeze to death?"

I stared at him, shocked he would say it out loud as though it was nothing. "Yes, I can see your point. I hope that's not what happened. Obviously."

"It's not obvious to me, Dr. Bancroft. Not at all." He wrote something else in that notebook of his, then brought it back to hold against his chest. "A lot of men put their wives and daughters in a place like this to keep them quiet or get them out of their lives. As a matter of fact, many of the prisoners in places like these are not insane."

"That may be true in other places, but Mrs. Mason wouldn't admit someone who didn't need to be here. She helps these poor people. Believe me, I looked at a few other facilities before choosing this one. This one was by far the most compassionate toward the patients."

"How is it you afford the fees for this place and an apartment for your...friend?"

"My father left me a great deal of money," I said. "He died when I was young."

"In the arms of his mistress, isn't that right?"

My mouth fell open once again. "How did you know that?"

"I had some time to look into you before you arrived this morning," Wallace said. "The more I learned, the more interested I became in you. As a suspect."

"Right." Sweat had broken out on my hairline. I reached into my pocket for my handkerchief. A sweaty brow would make me look guilty, but I couldn't seem to control my nerves. I'd never been interrogated by the police before.

"Tell me more about your brother-in-law," Wallace said. "Do you think he's involved in any way?"

"You mean if it turns out I'm innocent?" Innocent. We didn't even know that she'd passed away.

"Correct. I'd like to understand his relationship with you. Are you friendly?"

"Very much so. He's at my house often."

"Why is he leaving the country?" Wallace asked.

Good Lord. Was there anything this man didn't know?

And how was I going to explain why he was leaving the country without involving the Sullivans? The last thing I needed was Sean Sullivan's wrath unleashed upon my family.

"Let me help you," Wallace said. "I know Stella Wainwright is Sean Sullivan's daughter."

"You do?" How did he know this? The man was not like any cop I'd ever met before. Not that I'd met very many, but he seemed unusually clever.

"Yes, and I'm also aware of Sullivan's illegal business endeavors." He paused, setting aside his notebook and placing his hands over his belly. The buttons on his jacket strained against the ampleness of his midsection.

"I see." What else could I say? I had to stay calm or risk even further scrutiny.

"And what I know about Mr. Sullivan is that he's not hesitant to order hits on anyone he wants out of the way."

"Why would he care about my wife?" How strange that Wallace had become suspicious of Sullivan, just as Stella had. Were they right? Had Sullivan done something to Mary? As unhappy as I'd been the years since Mary's mind had gone to a dark place and not returned, I shuddered to think of her hurt or suffering.

"He wants his daughter to be happy. It's not inconceivable that he decided to get your current wife out of the way so that your mistress could take her place."

I shook my head, unable to utter a response even if I'd known what to say.

"What do you think about that theory?" Wallace asked, clearly not willing to let it go.

"I think that Sullivan has no idea of what's between me and his daughter. They're essentially estranged. He would not put the pieces together. And anyway, from what Stella says, he has no interest in being a loving father to her. She had not seen him for months until he showed up asking questions about her sister's whereabouts."

We were interrupted by a knock on the door. Wallace shouted to come in and a man dressed in a cop uniform entered.

"Sir. There's something you should see," he said to Wallace.

My stomach dropped.

Wallace nodded toward me. "Dr. Bancroft, stay here."

"What's happened?" I heard myself asking as if I were speaking down a long tunnel.

Neither man replied, hurrying out the door and leaving me behind, too stunned and heartsick and imagining the worst to move.

———

I DON'T KNOW how long I waited for the chief to return. The wintry light through the windows gave me no indication of how much time had passed. I couldn't sit, pacing around the small room with only my frayed nerves to keep me company.

Finally, I wandered out of the office and down the hallway, past several other offices, until I came into the great room, where the patients spent leisure time. Today, it was as if nothing unusual were going on. Patients stood at easels painting, played games in small groups, or read in cozy chairs. If I hadn't known better, I would have thought I'd happened upon a social club of some kind.

I asked one of the nurses if she had any idea where the police chief was. She nodded toward the lawn, where there were several policemen roaming about. "What are they doing?"

"I couldn't say, sir." The nurse hurried away, clearly hoping to avoid further questions.

I buttoned up my coat and headed outside. They couldn't keep me imprisoned in the office. I scanned the yard for Mrs. Mason and found her under one of the awnings speaking to a secretary. I called out to her as I made my way toward them. She met my gaze, a look of panic on her face.

"Dr. Bancroft, you should go inside," Mrs. Mason said. "I'll take you back to my office."

"Why can't I be out here?"

"Because—"

She didn't get to finish whatever it was she was going to say because we were interrupted by a shout, followed by the barking of hounds some distance away.

"Oh dear." Mrs. Mason sucked in her cheeks. "Please, allow me to take you inside."

"What is it?" I didn't wait to hear what she had to say, taking off in the direction of the shouting.

I raced across the icy grass toward the thicket of trees. After a time, I came upon a group of people, several of them in cop uniforms, gathered around something on the ground.

It only took me a moment to realize it was a body. Mary's body?

I broke through the crowd, gathered around, and saw that it was indeed my wife. She'd been torn apart by an animal, her innards on display. I cried out, then fell to my knees.

One of the cops rushed over to me. "Dr. Bancroft, you don't want to see her like this."

"It's too late," I said. "What happened?"

"We're not sure where she was killed, but an animal must have dragged her here. We'd searched this area earlier, and there was no sign of her. But please, you have to go inside and wait for the chief. Otherwise, I'm going to have to arrest you."

Numbly, I allowed him to manhandle me back inside, where a nurse agreed to take me to the office. I was shaking so badly by then I could barely stand. Being nearly pushed onto the sofa in Mason's office was actually a relief.

"I'll sit with you if that's all right?" I recognized the nurse from other interactions. For a moment, I searched for her name, but then it came to me. Agnes. She'd been employed here six years ago when I'd first brought Mary to asylum. She was silver-haired and slightly stooped but had lively, intelligent eyes. I'd always been under the impression that nothing much went on around here without her knowing about it.

"Yes, fine," I mumbled. "Why would anyone do this?"

"I don't know, Doctor. I surely don't. But we'll find out. The chief of police is a competent investigator if you can believe it. He'll discover who did this. I know he will."

"What if it's just that she somehow escaped and wandered into the woods? She wouldn't have understood how dangerous that would be in this weather."

"If that's the case, then they'll know. In the end, the truth always comes out."

Was that true? Who knew?

My last meal was threatening to come up. I stumbled to my feet and ran out into the hallway, desperately looking for a place to vomit. I remembered the restrooms, making it just in time to unleash the contents of my stomach into the toilet. Then, sweaty and still feeling sick, I sank to the cold floor. What now? What now?

BY NIGHTFALL, they'd brought my poor Mary's ravaged body inside to one of the examination rooms. The coroner arrived and disappeared behind the closed door. In the meantime, I waited. At some point, it occurred to me to call home. Mother would be worried and possibly frantic to hear an update.

Mrs. Mason allowed me to use the phone in her office. The operator put me through, and Mother's voice came through the receiver.

"Darling, I've been worried sick," Mother said. "Have they found her?"

I nodded as if she could see me. "She's dead. They found her body in the woods. It had been dragged there from somewhere else. Whether by animal or man, we do not know."

"Oh, Percy."

"They don't know if she wandered out to the woods, got lost, and froze to death, or if someone took her there and left, knowing she would be too confused to find her way back."

"It has to be the former. Why would anyone want her dead?"

"I don't know." Tears waited, hot behind my eyes. "I just don't know."

"When can you come home?"

"Not tonight. I need to stay to make arrangements to get her home, among other things." Like defending myself. "Also, they're trying to find Simon so they can question him. He was the last family member to visit her."

"Simon wouldn't do such a thing," Mother said. "Would he?"

"I don't know what motive he would have. No one has one but me."

For a moment, I heard only the crackle of static on the line. "Is that what they think? Because of Stella?"

"Yes. And Mother, he said cops will come by the house to speak with you and Stella. I'm afraid she's on the suspect list."

"Did they tell you that?"

"No, but if they think I have a motive, they'll think she does too."

"I'll have her stay here again tonight," Mother said. "That way, they can talk to both of us. She won't want to be alone."

I hung up after saying goodbye just as Wallace entered the office. He shut the door behind him. "We have something," Wallace said, sitting in one of the chairs next to Mrs. Mason's desk. "One of the staff admitted to seeing a woman with Mary just before she vanished."

"A woman? Someone other than a nurse?" I asked.

"That's right. He has no description of her face, because she was wearing a hat pulled down over her eyes and a scarf."

"Why didn't they find her last night? Surely they combed those woods?" I asked.

"The young man works here as one of the night guards. He was afraid to come forward. Instead of standing by the door, he was outside smoking a cigarette. But before he took his break, he noticed Mary huddled in the corner of the recreation room with a woman. He assumed it was a visitor. If the woman in question had anything to do with her disappearance, she must have taken the opportunity to sneak Mary out the door while the guard was otherwise occupied."

"Can't you check the visitor logs to find out who it was?"

"We did that. Mrs. Mason recognized the names of all the visitors from yesterday. Most visitors are family members, and she's familiar with them. She saw nothing unusual."

A woman.

For one horrific second, I thought about Mother. She'd been clear to me that she thought I should seize love, even if it meant going outside my marriage vows. It was her opinion that my marriage was essentially over and that I should feel free to move on. Specifically with Stella. Yet I could not entertain such an idea. I would not be my father.

But what if Mother took it upon herself to give me the life I wanted so desperately with Stella? All my life, Mother had been my protector and my champion. I had no doubt she would do anything for me. But this? Murder? Of her own daughter-in-law? In my wildest imagination, I could not see her doing anything so heinous. Not even to give me the freedom to find love again.

What about for Clara? My mother was getting older. Perhaps she worried about what would become of Clara should she pass away. She knew how much Clara wished for Stella to become her mother. Had that pushed Mother into doing something unthinkable?

No, it couldn't be. Like me, Mother abhorred violence of any kind. Not to mention that she would not risk going to prison or being put to death. For one thing, she knew Clara and I needed her.

My next horrid thought was Stella. But no. Like Mother, she'd been with us for most of the day. There was no way she could have taken the train up yesterday afternoon and returned in time for dinner.

"Do you have any idea about who this mystery woman could be?" Wallace asked, pulling me from my morbid thoughts.

"No sir, I don't. Both my mother and Stella were with me yesterday afternoon."

His thick mustache quivered as he peered at me through his small, deep-set eyes. "I suppose you have countless servants who will back up your story?"

"We do indeed." I scratched behind one ear, trying to think of a way to convince him that we had nothing to do with this.

He tapped his fingers on the arm of his chair. "This marriage has been a burden to you?"

"Burden's not the right word. Has it been exceedingly difficult? Yes. Am I lonely? Yes. Would I like to move on with my life, remarry, and perhaps have more children? Only if I knew that Mary had no hope of getting better. It seemed clearer and clearer every month that my wife would not return to me. Not as the woman she'd once been, anyway. She'd been violent toward me and our infant daughter, Chief. I couldn't keep her with me and sleep at night. But did I wish her dead? Especially in such a horrifying way? Never. She was my wife. I can still remember what she was like before she lost this battle with her mind. I could not harm her. Not the mother of my child and the woman I promised to take care of in sickness and in health."

"I suppose you'd like to go home?" Wallace asked.

"Not until I have her body to take with me. Her family has a plot where her brother would like her laid to rest."

"Speaking of Simon Price—he's been located and brought into the precinct for questioning."

"It's not Simon," I said. "He was nothing but devoted to her."

We were interrupted by one of the deputies, who said he needed Wallace. "Do you have a place to stay?" Wallace asked me.

"Mrs. Mason said I can sleep here on her couch," I said. "Which I will do."

"The coroner should be done with his work by tomorrow," Wallace said. "You should make arrangements for a casket and a burial."

Before I could answer, he was gone.

For a moment, I remained seated, my body suddenly as limp as a rag doll. Mary was dead. After all her suffering and the hardship of my little family, she was gone. How was I supposed to feel? Was this numbness normal, or did it prove once and for all that I was a monster? Because just under the surface lay relief.

9

ESTELLE

Mrs. Bancroft stood in the doorway of the sitting room, her complexion ashen and her hands trembling. I rushed to her and drew her over to the sofa, encouraging her to sit.

"I've heard from Percy."

I waited, holding my breath.

"They found Mary's body. She froze to death and was then attacked by some kind of wild animal. Or at least, that's their initial conclusion."

I held on to the back of a chair, afraid I might faint, as black dots danced before my eyes. "The poor woman," I whispered. "Who would do this?"

"I have to believe it was an accident," Mrs. Bancroft said. "She wandered outside for whatever reason her addled brain would give her and got lost. With the weather as it is, it wouldn't take long for her to freeze to death."

"How will we ever know?"

"The police are doing a thorough investigation. Percy said to expect them to come by tonight or tomorrow to question us."

"I don't know what to say. Or think."

"Me either," Mrs. Bancroft said. "I have to tell Clara."

"Not yet. Not until Percival returns."

"Yes, yes. It can wait, I suppose."

"May I get you something?" I asked.

"A sherry, please."

My own hands shook as I poured us each a small glass and returned to the sitting area in front of the fire.

No sooner had we settled in than Robert announced a visitor. "It's Mr. Price, ma'am. Shall I show him in?"

"Yes, please," Mrs. Bancroft said, her gaze darting toward me.

Simon appeared, looking frazzled and grief-stricken, with red eyes and wild hair, as if he'd spent the last hour running his hands through the dark strands.

"Simon?" Mrs. Bancroft got to her feet. "I suppose by the look on your face, I can assume you've heard."

"Yes, the police questioned me. I came right over afterward."

"May I get you a drink?" I asked.

He scowled at me. "I'll get my own."

"Allow me, sir," Robert said.

He knew how to blend into the scenery so well that I'd forgotten he was there.

"What did they want from you?" Mrs. Bancroft asked after Simon had sat and taken what appeared to be a fortifying drink of his whiskey.

"They asked me a lot of questions about my whereabouts yesterday." He took another drink. "This is unthinkable." Tears filled his eyes, and despite our differences, I felt terribly sorry for him.

"I'm sorry," I said. "Truly."

He glared at me through narrowed eyes. "Did you have anything to do with this? Was it you? Don't deny this gives you what you want."

I felt the color drain from my face. "I would never do another person harm if I could help it. Anyway, I was here all day and night with Mrs. Bancroft and Percival. The staff can tell you that it's so."

He stared at me for a while longer and then shrugged, as if I didn't matter enough to acknowledge. I knew better. Inside, he seethed with anger.

"Stella had nothing to do with this...unfortunate tragedy," Mrs. Bancroft said.

"If you say so," Simon said, bitterness dripping from his mouth like coffee left on the stove too long.

"What did the police ask you?" Mrs. Bancroft asked.

"They wanted to know why I was there yesterday and what time I left and on and on. I was on the train home when she supposedly disappeared and had a ticket to prove it. For now, they let me go. But, Miss Sullivan, they know everything that happened between our two families. They implied that this may be related to my father's involvement in organized crime."

"As in, revenge from a warring family?" Mrs. Bancroft asked, sitting forward slightly.

"Something like that." Simon got up and went to the liquor cabinet to pour himself another drink. "They told me not to leave the country until they're further along in their investigation. I'm afraid Sullivan's going to kill me, and the cops may jail me."

"You must stay here with us," Mrs. Bancroft said. "We'll keep you safe."

"I don't have much choice. Not with Sullivan's thugs and the cops suspecting I killed my own sister." His voice cracked, and he dropped his face into his hands.

"What if they're right?" I asked. "What if this does have something to do with our families' rivalries? My father's vengeful. He might have done this to further punish you." I hated to say out loud the words that I feared were the truth, but it had to be said. I'd learned my lessons about lies. It was better to say the truth than hide within your lies. Eventually, they always came to light.

"Is your father really so cruel?" Mrs. Bancroft asked.

"That's been proven," Simon said.

"I have to agree with you." I kept my voice matter-of-fact. The less emotion I showed Simon, who still felt very much my enemy, the better.

Mrs. Bancroft nodded and then seemed to speak her thoughts out loud as they came to her. "They appear to have taken more interest in this than they typically would—that is, for a mental patient to freeze to death in the woods not far from her asylum's grounds wouldn't normally get this much attention."

"You're right," Simon said. "No one cares about the poor souls trapped in that place."

"Given that, it would make sense they think it's related to your fathers," Mrs. Bancroft said.

"Was this supposed to be a message to me?" Simon asked.

"One my father thought the authorities wouldn't care about?" I asked, also speaking my thoughts as they entered my mind. "Less likely to gather attention but a sure way to let us know he's out there, controlling us. Sending clear instructions to stay out of his business.

"Simon, he threatened Percival and had Clara and me followed. Maybe he thought it wasn't enough to get your attention and decided to kill your sister." By the time I finished this thought, tears leaked from my eyes. How could my father have done such a thing? We'd all gotten the message. Simon was supposed to leave for Europe tomorrow.

What had I told my father? Had I somehow given him information that helped in his decision?

Robert came in then to tell us the police detectives were here. Mrs. Bancroft and I immediately rose to our feet. "Show them into the study," she said to Robert.

"Yes ma'am."

"Simon, go up to the guest room and wait for them to leave," Mrs. Bancroft said. "There's no reason they need to know you're here."

For once, he did as suggested.

IT WAS ONLY one detective who waited for Mrs. Bancroft and me in the study. Tall and lanky, with a head that brought to mind a watermelon, he was named Forsyth.

He greeted us politely and then asked Mrs. Bancroft if he might speak to me alone. She gave my hand a reassuring squeeze before leaving us.

"Please sit," Forsyth said. "I have a few questions for you. Shouldn't take long."

"I'm here to help."

"How long have you known the Bancrofts?"

"Since last fall. I was unwell, and they were kind enough to take me in."

"Is Percival Bancroft a benefactor or your lover?" He asked this in a calm, almost soothing voice that normally would lull me into a sleepy state. However, I was much too nervous to be lulled into anything.

"He's only my benefactor," I said. "After all, he's a married man. He takes care of me out of the kindness of his heart."

"He puts you up in an apartment simply because he's kind?" The detective, as mild-mannered as he appeared, had a gaze that could fell a large tree with its intensity.

I sighed, having grown tired of this question. "That's correct." I went on to explain that I helped Mrs. Bancroft with her work. "After she nursed me back to health, that is."

"A woman such as yourself, devoting hours to the poor—it's somewhat unusual, is it not?"

"I was only too happy to do something useful with my time."

The usual questions followed. Where was I yesterday and so forth. I detailed the time in question without hesitation. He scribbled it into a small notebook with a pencil.

Forsyth looked up from his writing to say, "One of the employees at the asylum has confessed to seeing Mrs. Bancroft —that is, Mary Bancroft—in the company of a woman he didn't recognize just minutes before her disappearance. He was outside having a cigarette instead of keeping watch at the door. Before he knew it, she'd vanished. As had the woman with her. He couldn't see the woman's face, given she wore a large-brimmed hat and scarf."

"Was she wearing a coat?" I don't know what made me ask such a question, but it fell out of my mouth.

Forsyth flipped through his notes, clearly taken during another interview. "Yes. The employee believes the coat was an ordinary brown, with a matching hat. The scarf was purple." His brow wrinkled. "Or rather, lavender, to be more precise."

"That is very specific."

"Does it bring to mind anything or anyone?" Forsyth asked. "As in, do you know anyone who wears a lavender scarf?"

"I can't say that I do. However, my circles are rather small these days."

"What do you mean?"

"Other than the Bancrofts, I have little social activity. My family and I no longer...speak." That was the best way to say it.

"What do you mean? You're estranged?"

"Correct." I peered at him, curious about what he knew. Was he feigning ignorance? How much did he know about my father's business affairs? Or should I say, criminal affairs.

"Miss Sullivan, it would be best if you told me the truth in plain terms. Why are you no longer welcome in your father's home?"

"After the death of my fiancé and my subsequent...you know...condition, he didn't want anything to do with me."

He looked at me blankly. "Condition?"

Ah, he did not know about the baby. Should I tell him? It wasn't relevant to the murder of Mary Price Bancroft. May she rest in peace. Was she at peace now? I certainly hoped so.

Forsyth cleared his throat. "Miss Sullivan, my apologies for being blunt, but I need you to focus on my questions."

I startled, as if pulled from a trance. "Yes, I'm sorry."

"In addition, I need you to tell me everything. If I think you're hiding something, then it only strengthens my suspicions."

Suspicions. How could he think I would ever hurt anyone? Wasn't it obvious? "What do you want to know?"

"Your condition—to what do you refer?"

"I was pregnant." My mother would have cringed at the term. In polite circles, she always told us one should refer to it as "with child." All I knew was that my child was no longer with me.

God bless the detective. He had the decency to flush. So, he didn't know everything.

"My fiancé was killed right before he could propose. By then, I was already pregnant. My father and mother didn't take kindly to the shame I would bring to the family should it come out that I was to have a child out of wedlock. Thus, my sister and her husband agreed to take the baby. A little girl." I paused to swallow the lump that developed in the back of my throat.

"Are you aware of the ties your father has to organized crime?"

"Is that why you're so interested in Mary Bancroft's death?" It was my turn to be blunt. "Are you using it as a means to my father?"

"Why would you ask such a thing? Are they related?"

"I have no idea. What I do know is that my father's ties, as you so subtly put it, destroyed our family. My sister and her husband wanted nothing to do with his ways and moved far away."

"Why move?"

I stared at him, trying to decipher if he had an inkling that my father had killed Connie. What exactly did the police know? How many of them were in his pocket?

"My father wanted both my fiancé and Pierre to work for him. Neither wanted to. We suspect that Connie threatened to expose him by going to the police. Thus, Pierre didn't feel confident he could refuse without suffering the consequences."

Forsyth blinked, then cocked his head to the right. "Consequences. Are you saying you think your father ordered a hit on your fiancé?"

Despite everything, the idea of betraying my father seemed impossible. *Remember the grief and rage*, I reminded myself. He took everything from me. My love, my baby. He'd allowed me to nearly perish on the streets of New York City while he entertained his mobster friends and spent time with his mistress.

"It is my belief that my father's responsible for Constantine Harris's death." There, I said it. "I have no proof, nor does anyone else. Except for Mary Bancroft." Oh, my goodness. I hadn't connected that fact until this very moment. "She witnessed her father's killing and went mad not a month later. Simon Price, whom I gather you've already spoken to, believes the shock and grief of it all contributed greatly to her demise, in addition to giving birth. The psychosis appeared shortly after having Clara. She became violent, as I'm sure you know."

"Yes, ma'am."

I'd said too much. I could see it in his eyes. He'd come to a conclusion, false though it may be. I'd killed Mary Bancroft so that I could have her husband all to myself.

"I would never hurt anyone," I said softly. "Not after what I've been through. I'd never betray the people who have taken me in and treated me like family. You may think that Percival and I are intimate, but you're wrong."

"Forgive me if I find that hard to believe. It's rarely the case that people do the moral thing."

"You may think that, given your line of work, but that doesn't mean it's true. People, for the most part, are decent."

"You may be correct. But whether it's true of you and Dr. Bancroft has yet to be seen."

He said I could go and to send Mrs. Bancroft in to speak with him next. I agreed, leaving the room on legs that felt weak and wobbly and a stomach that churned with nerves.

PERCIVAL

Despite Wallace's instruction to stay put the night before, by the late afternoon, he'd said it was all right to return home so that I could begin to make funeral arrangements. Before I left, I spoke with Mrs. Mason about getting Mary's body back to the city so that I could bury her in her family's plot.

"We'll take care of everything," Mrs. Mason said.

"I can't thank you enough for your kindness. As horrific as this is, I can still appreciate everything you and your staff did to help Mary."

"It's very sad, no matter how you look at it."

"What do *you* think happened?" I asked. "Do you think it's possible an error was made by one of the staff? Perhaps a door left open on accident?"

"It's certainly possible." Mrs. Mason folded her hands on top of her desk and leaned forward slightly. "If it is, I'm absolutely devastated. On the other hand, it would be a better outcome than murder."

"Either way, she's gone."

"I know it's not been easy for you. You've been more loyal

and dedicated than most husbands, I can assure you. It's too soon for you to think about the future, of course, but I hope that when it's time, you'll allow yourself to love again. Perhaps make a new life with someone else. Have another child. You did your duty, Dr. Bancroft. Kept your vows. Do not let guilt or regret keep you from a joyful life."

Touched by her words, I thanked her again and then, with a heavy heart to keep me company, headed to the train station.

When I arrived home, the apartment was quiet. The women were probably dressing for supper upstairs. Clara would be about to have her supper with her nanny. I'd not bathed or changed clothes for what felt like forever. Thankfully, Robert ran a bath for me and laid out a suit for the evening by the time I'd undressed.

I gratefully sank into the hot water and closed my eyes. I had to tell Clara about her mother. The mother she'd never met. God, how had my life ended up this way?

I had not let myself think about Stella or what this meant for us. It was too much—the guilt and grief all swirled around like a tornado in my head. Until they figured out who did this to Mary, I could hardly think about the future. Although, what if they never discovered the truth?

My thoughts zigzagged back to Sean Sullivan. Was Stella right that he had something to do with this? Had he become nervous, Mary would somehow come to her right mind and tell the police what she'd witnessed the night of her father's murder. But even if she had, which was incredibly unlikely given her mental state, it still couldn't be pinned on him. He'd had a professional killer perform the ugly act. Unless the police had put together all the crumbs and clues of Sean Sullivan's criminal activity because of Mary's death?

I thought about Mary. The young woman I'd met and fallen in love with over seven years ago now. At times, I daydreamed about what my life would have been like if I'd chosen someone else. But it was not a long daydream because, without Mary, I wouldn't have Clara. Therefore, Mary and I could never be seen as only a mistake.

She'd been beautiful when I'd first met her, although the roots of instability were there if I were truly honest with myself. Paranoia, for one, seemed to plague her even before she had the breakdown. One night after a party, she'd been convinced someone was following us. In hindsight, now that I understood more about her father's ties to organized crime, it was clear she had good reason to be afraid. For all I knew, she might have been right. What had she seen before our marriage that had made her so sure there were reasons to be afraid?

I would never know.

Grief overtook me. I sank further into the warm, soapy water and gave in to my grief. I wept for Mary and for the life denied her. I wept for my little daughter, who would never know her mother. I even wept for myself—for the utter loneliness that had come from a marriage I'd entered with such hope, but that had ended with the kind of pain that lived within my bones. Memories of all the visits over the years merged into one long, sad tale of defeat. They'd pushed out all the good remembrances of a time when I thought I would live happily ever after with my bride.

But it was not to be. Now I was about to enter a new kind of life. One I hoped meant freedom to find happiness again and not the gallows. I had to have faith that the truth would come out one way or the other.

For now, I had to pull myself together. Clara must be told. The detectives would continue to lurk and ask questions of everyone in this household. I couldn't blame them. This situation pointed to my guilt, even if it were far from the truth. Still, I must remain hopeful that it would soon be obvious that both Stella and I had behaved morally and with sacrifice for the greater good.

What happened next? I could not say with certainty, other than I would be on my knees praying for us all.

———

AFTER I'D BATHED and dressed, I took myself down the hallway to Clara's nursery. She was there, already in her flannel nightgown, sitting on her small bed looking at a picture book.

"Papa," she shouted, bouncing off of the bed and into my arms.

I held her close, taking in the sweet scent of her hair and the warmth of her familiar bulk. How I loved her.

"Where were you all night?" Clara asked as I set her down.

I went to the window seat, patting the cushion next to me. "Come sit, sweetheart."

She scrambled up to sit beside me. "What is it, Papa? Has something happened?"

"I'm afraid it has." I rubbed my forehead, hoping to conjure just the right words. "Your mother's passed away. She's no longer with us."

"Where is she?"

"Heaven, I'm sure."

Clara searched my face with her round eyes. "What happened to her?"

"She somehow got outside in the cold and froze to death." I might as well tell her the truth. There was no reason to lie to her, although it was not necessary, she know about the animals who had gotten to her body.

"That's very sad, isn't it, Papa?"

"It is sad."

"I'm sad for her, but not for me. I didn't know her. Am I bad?"

"No, of course not. You cannot really mourn someone you didn't know." My voice broke, and I drew in a shaky breath.

She crawled into my lap. "I'm sorry, Papa. You loved her very much, didn't you?"

"I did. She gave me you, which I will always be grateful for."

"Even though I'm the one who made her sick?"

"You didn't make her sick," I said. "Whatever do you mean?"

"I heard the servants talk about it once. They said that having me made her sick."

"It was not you. She was ill. Please, do not give that another thought. She was sick long before you."

"Is it true she tried to hurt me?"

I closed my eyes against her gaze for just a second, the pain so intense I thought I might split apart. "She was not well, love. She didn't know what she was doing."

"All right." Clara rested her cheek against my chest. "Don't be sad, Papa. Now you can marry Stella."

I scrambled for the right words but came up with nothing. "The future will unfold as it should." It was a rather lame thing to say, but what could be uttered that didn't hold too many promises? It was no secret that Clara wished us to marry and become a family. The very last thing I wanted was for her to feel disappointed or be hurt by anything else the adults in her life had done.

"I know they will," Clara said in answer to my trite words. "I've known it for a long time."

I kissed the top of her head. "I love you. Don't ever forget it."

"I love you, Papa." She nestled closer. "Don't you ever forget it."

WHEN I WENT DOWNSTAIRS after tucking Clara in for the night, Stella was alone in the sitting room. The sight of her almost had me bursting into tears once again. She looked so normal sitting there with a book open on her lap and Charlie at her feet. The light from the fireplace lit up her dark hair but shadowed her face.

She must have heard me because she looked up from her book to greet me. "Percival, thank goodness you're back." She stood, setting aside her book. "Penelope brought Charlie over a few minutes ago. She said he was despondent without me. How are you?"

"I'm holding up," I said. "How about you? Mother said the police were here."

She nodded, returning to her chair before realizing she'd left the book open on the seat cushion. Flushing, she reached under her skirt to lift the book out from under her and set it on the table. "Yes, they were here for quite some time."

"Did the police say you were to stay here rather than return to your apartment?" I asked, leaning down to give Charlie a few pets.

"No, but your mother asked me to. She didn't want me alone, and frankly, I would much rather stay here, even with Mrs. Landry and Penelope there to keep me company."

"Will they be safe, do you think?"

"It's not them who interest my father. How are you doing?" Stella asked, sympathy softening her expression. "I'm so very sorry about what's happened."

Her compassion reminded my eyes of their recent tears. I fought their escape with everything I could muster. "I shall not soon rid myself of the image of her lifeless, ravaged body. She deserved so much better than what she got in this life."

"She's free now. Healed and whole in heaven."

"I hope you're right." I rubbed my eyes, feeling more weary than I ever had in my life.

"What can I do?" She fell before me, her skirts fanning out around her, and reached for me but pulled back at the last moment. Instead, she remained on the floor, staring up at me with beseeching eyes. "I'll do anything. Anything at all if it were to help you."

"There's nothing you can do for me but thank you," I said.

"I'm so afraid of what's to come. Either or both of us could be hauled to prison at any time. More likely me, as the person they think may have lured her outside was a woman. They might pin it on me, even though I have an alibi here at the house. They're anxious to find someone to blame. It's not much of a leap. Not really. After all, they think I have a motive."

Her confession startled me to my very core. Here I'd been thinking only of myself without realizing how terrified she must be. "I would never let that happen."

"How would you stop it?"

"I'd confess to it myself if it were to save you," I said.

"They wouldn't believe you. Or they'd think we were in on it together. Don't you see? They want to make me the villain. It's easier that way. An angry woman kills her lover's wife in a moment of rage and jealousy. That's a story everyone can understand. When something senseless like this happens, it's human nature to want to find a reason why. Something that makes sense."

"But you're not my lover." I stifled a shiver. The idea of holding her in my arms made me feel almost dizzy. What was wrong with me? My wife had just died.

"No, but everyone thinks I am." She placed her hand on the arm of my chair to help herself rise up from the floor and went to stand in front of the fire. "Anyway, I would never allow them to blame you. Clara needs you. As does your mother. No one needs me. No one would miss me for long."

"That's not true. I need you. I would miss you for the rest of my life should you be taken from me again."

She sank back into her chair, wringing her hands. "My family's caused yours enough pain. Doesn't it seem that I'm a plague upon your life?"

"None of this is your fault or your doing. Please, you must stop taking your father's sins upon yourself. You're innocent in all of this. Over and over, you've done what's right for everyone but yourself. We simply have to get through the next few weeks and have faith that the truth about Mary's killer will come out. Also, we mustn't forget—it may have been an accident. A lapse in care at the asylum, and she walked out the door of her own volition."

For a moment, I sat there, thinking through the different scenarios. It seemed to me that one of the staff had to have been involved. Had they been offered money in exchange for their assistance?

My thoughts were interrupted when Robert came in to announce that the police were here. Before I could even gather my thoughts and instruct Robert to show them in, the officers had already forced their way into our sitting room, their heavy boots echoing on the polished wooden floor. The lead officer, a burly man with a stern expression, stepped forward, his eyes scanning the room with an intensity that made my heart race.

"What do you want?" I demanded, rising from my seat, but my voice wavered, betraying my fear.

The officer ignored my question, his gaze settling on Stella, who stood frozen by the fire, her complexion alabaster white. "Estelle Sullivan," he announced, his voice cold and authoritative, "you are under arrest for the murder of Mary Bancroft."

The words hung heavy in the air. Stella's face contorted in a mixture of shock and disbelief.

"This is wrong," I said. "She couldn't have done this. She was with me the entire evening."

No one seemed to listen. It was as if I were not in the room. One of the officers twisted her arms behind her back and clicked cold steel handcuffs into place. Stella winced, her gaze locking with mine.

Charlie, sensing his beloved owner in distress, growled and

then barked. I'd never heard him make more than a peep, but Stella had never been in danger before.

"I'll hire an attorney," I said to Stella. "Don't worry. We'll get this sorted."

The lead officer turned to me, his eyes devoid of any empathy. "Let's go."

Charlie's barking grew even more frantic as he tried to follow Stella, but an officer held him back.

"It's all right, Charlie," Stella said. "Stay with Percival."

Charlie sank to the floor by my feet, whining.

Stella did not struggle but went meekly, turning only once to look back at me. The expression in her eyes broke my heart. Defeat, they said.

I stood there, helpless and horrified, as they marched her out of the room. Seconds later, the front door slammed shut behind them. Robert stood beside me, equally stunned, his face ashen.

"This is wrong," I whispered, more to myself than to him, my mind racing to piece together the nightmare that had just unfolded.

Charlie returned to my side, whimpering and looking at the door with sad, confused eyes. I knelt down and stroked his fur, trying to calm him as much as myself. "It's going to be okay, Charlie. We'll find a way to help her," I murmured, though my voice lacked conviction.

I swept Charlie into my arms and sank back into my chair. I wasn't sure which of us was trembling harder, me or the dog. Stella, accused of such a heinous crime—it was inconceivable. What evidence did they have? None whatsoever.

"Robert, call my attorney. Ask him to meet me at the jailhouse."

"Yes sir."

I'd do whatever it took to save her—no matter the time or cost. Stella's life depended on it.

11

ESTELLE

My breath formed clouds in the frigid night air as I was thrown into the police wagon. I shivered, as they had not given me time to don a coat before hauling me out of the apartment.

At the police station, I was escorted inside the warm lobby, a bustling hub of activity with officers milling about and suspects being processed. The air was thick with the scent of tobacco smoke and sweat.

I was led to a wooden desk where an officer, his face a mask of disinterest, began the routine.

"Name?" he barked, his pen poised over a large, worn ledger.

"Estelle Sullivan," I replied, my voice barely a whisper.

The officer jotted down my name and then proceeded with a litany of questions. Age, address, place of birth—all documented meticulously. My fingerprints were taken, black ink staining my fingers like the damnation of a scarlet letter.

Next, a matronly woman with a stern expression led me to a small, dimly lit room where I was instructed to change into a plain, coarse prison dress. My clothes were taken away, folded, and stored as evidence. The material scratched against my skin, a constant reminder of my newfound reality.

The stone walls of the jailhouse itself felt like the inside of a cold hell. Bars lined the corridors, each cell with only a narrow cot, a thin blanket, and a small bucket for sanitation. The dim lighting cast long shadows, making me feel as if someone would jump out from the darkness.

I was placed in a cell near the end of the corridor. As the heavy door clanged shut behind me, I collapsed onto my cot and allowed myself to sob. How could I have expected anything else? My life was a series of tragedies. Would it end with a rope around my neck?

The cold seeped through the thin walls, and the lightweight blanket offered little warmth. I curled into a ball, shivering and praying for a miracle in equal measure. Occasionally, I heard the distant sounds of the city—carriages clattering over cobblestones. Life went on without me. It would go on without me. This was it, I thought. The end. I'd been on borrowed time, perhaps, since the birth of Mireille. I should have died in those days after leaving my sister and Pierre. Instead, Percival had found me and tried to rescue me, but it was not to be. I was doomed. I'd brought nothing but trouble to the Bancrofts, including Mary's murder. I had no doubt my father had something to do with it. He'd be only too happy to let me take the fall for it.

Had he done it simply to get rid of me once and for all? If I were in prison, he would not have to worry about me making trouble for him.

Would Percival and his mother and little Clara be convinced I was guilty? Although I was with them during the night in question, the cops could make an argument that I'd hired someone to kill her. After all, if my father had done this, he would have hired someone. Thus, it was not hard to believe that

I would have done the same. I had the motive. I loved a married man. Getting rid of her would give me what I wanted.

A jury wouldn't know my heart. They wouldn't believe a woman like me, with nothing left to lose, could possibly be innocent. The prosecutor would make a solid case against me. A baby out of wedlock, and feeling as if I had no choice but to give her to my sister. All of which was enough to break me, they might say, but then I fell in love with my benefactor, plunging further into immorality. They would paint me as a woman accustomed to fine living who believed my only hope was to attach myself to the Bancrofts permanently. The only way to do that? Get rid of the wife. It would not be hard to make a jury believe it to be true.

Would Percival believe it too?

Not that. I could bear being hanged for a crime I didn't commit as long as he and Mrs. Bancroft believed me.

I fell asleep at some point, waking in the early morning to gray light filtering through the tiny window. I heard a commotion at the end of the corridor. Footsteps approached, and the heavy door creaked open to reveal a guard carrying a tray containing a lukewarm porridge and weak cup of coffee.

Although I wasn't hungry and the porridge was barely edible, I managed a few bites. If I were to be questioned again, I needed the energy to answer clearly.

Mortified, I used the bucket to urinate. Did the guard come to take it later, or would my cell now smell of urine?

I started to cry again, huddled on the bed. I wasn't strong enough or brave enough to face what was to come. It would be better if I were to die now. Could I use the blanket as a noose?

The guard arrived to take my tray and to my relief, the bucket. A few minutes later, he returned, his keys jangling as he unlocked the door. "You have a visitor," he said, his voice gruff but not all together unkind.

My heart leapt with hope. "Who is it?"

"No idea, ma'am. I only follow orders. Could be your attorney, I reckon."

He didn't say anything further; he simply guided me out of the cell and down a hallway that led to a private room. To my relief, it was Percival waiting for me. Beside him was a man I didn't recognize, middle-aged and serious looking, with salt-and-pepper hair. His intense green eyes settled on me, sizing me up. In those eyes, I saw a man with a past, a man who had seen many things, most of them ugly.

No doubt, this was an attorney.

Percival had brought him to me. He still believed in my innocence. I said a silent prayer of thanks.

The room was stark, a plain table and chairs the only furnishings. The guard gestured for me to sit, and I did, my hands clasped tightly in my lap.

I gazed at Percival, drinking him in as if he were clear mountain water and I had just walked across the desert. He looked worn, with worry etched into his handsome features. "Are you all right? Have they hurt you?" Percival asked.

"I'm fine." My voice wobbled, but I didn't have it in me to act brave. "It's cold and scary, but I got through the night."

Percival introduced me to William Whitman. "He's one of the finest defense attorneys in the city. I spoke to my family attorney, and he referred me to Mr. Whitman. Thankfully, he's agreed to take your case."

"Thank you for coming," I said to Mr. Whitman.

Whitman sat down across from me, opening a leather briefcase and pulling out a notepad. Percival took the seat beside him, his hand reaching across the table to squeeze mine reassuringly.

For the next twenty minutes, I answered Whitman's questions, going over everything that I'd already told the police. We went through the night in question, covering my alibi and those who could vouch for my whereabouts.

Mr. Whitman nodded, seemingly satisfied with my answers. "Can you think of any details you can recall about that evening? What did you talk about at dinner?"

"Why do you need to know that?" I asked.

"Because the prosecution will know that Percival and you have a personal relationship. One that would give you a clear motive. Meaning the two of you could have been in on it together. The more details you remember, the better."

I recounted the dinner and the conversation. "Clara was there. She was allowed to stay up late because of the holiday."

"What was served for dinner?" Whitman asked.

For a moment, I couldn't remember.

"Breathe," Percival said.

"Yes, right." It all came back to me in a flood of images. "Roast beef. Potatoes dripping with butter." I added in as many of the dishes as I could. "I stuffed myself."

"You'd been living quite lean before this, isn't that right?" Whitman asked. "Tell me about those weeks. The ones you spent away from the Bancrofts."

I did so. Some of the details I hadn't shared with Percival. Several times, he flinched at my description of the destitution I faced.

Whitman listened intently, his pen moving swiftly across the page. I found myself wondering if he ever smiled. Typically I would have felt intimidated by him, but I was too tired and discouraged to feel anything of the sort.

Seemingly satisfied with my answers, Whitman looked up, his green eyes piercing. "The prosecution is going to argue that you hired someone to kill Mary. They'll claim you had a motive because of your relationship with Percival. We need to prepare for this angle."

I felt a surge of panic, even though I'd already guessed this would be their tactic.

"Do you have any financial records?" Whitman asked. "From the bank."

"I don't. I don't have any money," I said. "Even if I did, I wouldn't be able to use a bank without a husband."

"Right, good. That will help us," Whitman said.

"Unless they say I gave it to her," Percival said.

"They must not think you were involved," Whitman said. "Or you would be arrested as well."

As the meeting drew to a close, Whitman stood, gathering his notes and briefcase. "Miss Sullivan, you must stay strong. In my experience, the truth usually comes out. Don't give up faith."

I nodded, feeling a glimmer of hope for the first time since my arrest. "Thank you, Mr. Whitman. I'll do my best."

"They have a very weak case," Whitman said. "But I have a feeling something else is going on here."

"What do you mean?" I asked.

"Your father's a powerful man in the underworld of this fine city. They may be after him, not you."

"For her murder?" I asked.

"No, for his activities in organized crime. He's been under scrutiny for some time." Whitman stuffed his notepad into his briefcase.

"I was told he had the police department in his pocket," I said.

Whitman snapped his briefcase closed. "That may be so, but there's a new district attorney, and he's not afraid to take the whole ring down. In fact, that's what he wants."

The guard returned, saying it was time for me to return to my cell.

"I tried to get you out on bail, but they declined my request," Percival said, taking my hands. "I'm sorry."

"It means so much you believe in my innocence. If you thought I'd done this, I couldn't bear it."

"Don't be ridiculous. I know you," Percival said. "I'm going to

see your father and mother. He should know they've imprisoned you for a crime you didn't commit."

"You won't get anywhere. He doesn't care about me. Not
more than money, anyway."

"We'll see about that." Percival kissed my hand. "I won't give
up on you. Not ever."

I breathed in the scent of him before the guard led me away
and back to my cell. The remembrance of his scent and touch
might be enough to sustain me through another day and cold
night. Or would it?

PERCIVAL

I went first to Mr. Sullivan's apartment in the city, but his staff informed me that he'd returned to his house in Litchfield. Hearing this, I immediately bought a train ticket and headed north. A cab took me to the grand estate, dropping me at the front entrance. A butler answered the door.

"Good afternoon, I'm Dr. Percival Bancroft, here to see Mr. Sullivan. He's not expecting me."

The butler glared at me for a moment before asking me to wait in the foyer. "I'll see if he's available."

He returned minutes later, asking me to follow him into the library. To my surprise, it was not Mr. Sullivan waiting for me but Mrs. Sullivan. She was slight and fair and had this way of looking at me that seemed as if she were bracing herself for a punch in the face. I'd seen women like this before during my work. They were the wives of men who hit them or verbally lacerated them.

"Forgive me for calling on you unannounced," I said after introducing myself.

"You're Estelle's friend." Mrs. Sullivan nodded, looking me up and down. "I met your mother the other day. You favor her."

"I've heard that before."

"Please sit. May I offer you tea?"

"No, thank you. I don't want to cause any trouble."

"What can I do for you?"

"Stella's been arrested for the murder of my wife, Mary Bancroft."

"Your wife's dead?"

I told her what had happened and the subsequent suspicion that had come our way. "They're under the impression that there is something untoward between Stella and me, which is patently untrue. They've arrested Stella for the murder of my wife." I figured it was best to say it as plainly as possible. "I've come to let you know, as well as ask your husband a few questions."

"He's out hunting today." She folded her hands together in her lap in the same way I'd seen Stella do on occasion. "What would you like to ask him?"

"Stella's under the impression he may have ordered the death of my wife."

Mrs. Sullivan's bottom lip quivered. "Why would he do that? What possible motive would he have? He doesn't know you or your wife. Late wife."

"As I'm sure you're aware, there's a history between your family and Mary's. Stella believes he wants to make sure the death of Mr. Price is not linked back to him somehow. Are you aware he's having my family followed?"

"It's rather like him, isn't it?" She looked away, but not before I saw the deep pain reflected in her eyes.

"They're going to hang her for this, and she's innocent."

"How can you be so sure of her innocence?" She peered at me with an expression of curiosity but also skepticism.

"None of it makes sense. She was with my family during the time in question. My mother, my daughter, and our entire staff know it. As far as hiring someone to do it—like your husband

WHEN STARS RISE AT MIDNIGHT

would do—it would require money, of which she has none." I badly wanted to lambaste her for how hard it had been for Stella since she'd left this house. How good it would feel to chastise her for abandoning her daughter.

"It was her idea." Mrs. Sullivan wrung her hands. "To give the baby away, I mean. I think."

"Is that true?"

"Yes. No one made her do it. No one's ever been able to make Estelle do anything she didn't want to do. Estelle knew her decision was the right one for the baby. My daughter Mauve was made to be a mother. Estelle knew that."

"Do you not have any guilt at all?" I couldn't help but ask the question. "She almost died. Multiple times. Are your motherly instincts intact, Mrs. Sullivan?"

"Believe me, Dr. Bancroft, I have the guilt of a thousand mothers upon my shoulders. But I've been punished for my mistakes, I can assure you. I've been left with no one."

"Other than your husband."

"As I said, no one." The tone of her voice took me aback. I'm not sure I'd heard such utter despair in another's tone ever in my life. I hoped never to witness it again, for it made my heart ache, even as the anger toward this woman who would have let her own daughter die on the streets of New York City remained.

"They think the two of you are in love," Mrs. Sullivan said. "And that's the reason she wanted your wife dead?"

"That seems to be it, yes."

"Are you in love with her?"

I didn't answer for a moment, completely flummoxed by her direct question. My instinct was to brush it away with a dismissive gesture, but something else took over instead. For whatever reason, it was suddenly important that Stella's mother knew her daughter was loved. They may have discarded her, but my family had welcomed her into our lives with open arms. "My mother and daughter love her. And I love her too. However, you must believe me when I say we have remained chaste."

"Because you're married?"

"That's correct."

"She told me the same thing, which I found hard to believe then as I do now. Yet you seem to be an extraordinary man, Dr. Bancroft. But tell me, are you broken up about your wife's death, or does it come as a convenience to you?"

"The mother of my child has suffered greatly over the years, which grieves me no end. And yes, her death allows me a second chance at happiness with someone else. But I could never hurt another human being, especially one I loved with all my heart. It is hardest to say goodbye to those who we know have suffered so on earth. Now I must do so."

"That is so. I hope you believe she's now free and without suffering."

"I pray it is true," I said.

"I'll let my husband know you called upon us and the unfortunate news of Estelle's arrest. But I cannot promise he will do anything. That's why you've come, isn't it? For money for her defense?"

"I'm happy to take care of that," I said. "It's not money I came for but answers."

"I know my husband better than anyone, and although he's guilty of many heinous crimes, he would not have a young, very sick woman killed. If he did so, he would certainly not frame his own daughter for the murder. Is that what she thinks?"

"To be perfectly frank, she's in such a state of confusion and fear that she has no idea what to think. Mrs. Sullivan, she's gone through so much, lost so much. This is just another blow to her already tragic life."

"Don't you think I know that?"

I shrugged.

"I'll do what I can to rectify the situation." Mrs. Sullivan stood. "After all this is done, I wish you a happy life with my daughter. I hope you can make a new family."

I rose to my feet as well. "My daughter loves her and wishes very much for us to marry."

"She doesn't know her mother, then?"

"I'm afraid not," I said. "She's been too sick for me to expose Clara. It was never certain what she might do or say. She was violent, or I might have been able to take care of her myself."

"I'm sorry for your troubles, Dr. Bancroft. Truly, I am. Please, keep me informed."

"I'll do that. Would you let your husband know I'm still interested in speaking with him?"

Framed in the doorway, she hesitated, her fingers worrying the sleeve of her dress. "I would be remiss if I didn't advise you to stay away from my husband. He's like a lion. Challenge brings out the worst in him. I don't want anyone else to get hurt."

"I'll take that under advisement. Thank you for your time."

"Take care of yourself. And my daughter, God willing." The butler had appeared, hovering just a few feet away. "James, will you have one of the staff take Dr. Bancroft back to the train station?"

"Right away, ma'am." James hurried off.

"Good day, Dr. Bancroft."

I bade her farewell and headed out of the grand front entrance to wait for either a car or a carriage, hoping it wouldn't take long, as it was cold and I was anxious to return to my mother and Clara. Mother had been beside herself when I told her what had happened. She would be pacing the floor. The sooner I returned, the better.

13

ESTELLE

After a lunch of watery potato soup and a stale roll, I lay on my cot in my jail cell, wishing I could shut off my worried mind. I was about to ask the guard if he had any books lying around when he came to fetch my lunch tray.

"You have another visitor," he said.

I leapt to my feet. "Who is it?"

"A Mrs. Bancroft."

The sound of her name almost started me weeping, even though it seemed impossible to have more moisture still left to spring from my tear ducts.

I followed the guard back to the room I'd been in earlier with the attorney and Percival. Mrs. Bancroft was already on her feet by the time I arrived. She wasted no time pulling me into a fierce embrace.

"Darling girl, are you holding up? Have they harmed you in any way?"

"No, I'm fine. The food's terrible, but at least there is some."

We sat across the table from each other as the guard left us alone in the locked room.

"How's Clara?" I asked. "I've been so worried."

"She's resilient, so you mustn't worry about that. Because she doesn't know her mother, Mary's death has not been as hard as one might think. Clara wishes for you to return to us, however. She sent you this." Mrs. Bancroft pulled an envelope from her bag and handed it to me. "It was dictated to her nanny, but she signed her name."

"I'll save it for later," I said. "Something to help pass the time."

"Speaking of which, I brought you the book you had open on the coffee table as well as two others I thought you might enjoy." She slid them toward me. "The ghastly guard looked through my bag as if I might be carrying a gun. Can you imagine?"

"They think I'm a murderer, so it's less hard to envision than I would have thought possible."

"Dearest, what are we to do? I've been frantic with worry."

"I wish I knew. We have to pray they find the real killer. Is the funeral planned?"

"We will lay her to rest in her family plot, as were Simon's wishes."

"He must hate me," I said.

"Simon? No, he knows you didn't do it."

"Really?"

"Simon loved his sister, but he's a rational man. He knows you were with us that night and that your limited funds would not give you the opportunity to hire someone. None of us can understand how the police don't see the obvious."

"The lawyer thought they might actually be after Father. They're using me as a way to get to him."

"That theory's not without merit."

"If they think he cares enough to help me, they're wrong. He'll be glad to have me out of the way."

"How is it possible? A father should naturally love his daughter."

"I've vexed him all my life," I said. "And he didn't love me enough to spare the man I loved, so really, can we be surprised?"

The guard entered, saying our time was up.

Mrs. Bancroft hugged me tightly. "Do not despair. There will be a way to prove your innocence. I have to believe that, and you should too."

"I'll do my best." I picked up the novels from the table before turning to the guard. "I'm ready."

I held the books against my chest as he slammed the door to my cell shut, leaving me alone once more.

I sat on my cot and pulled the paper from the envelope to read Clara's note.

Dear Stella,

I miss you. I hope you're coming home soon. Today I played with my dollhouse and wished you were there to play with me. Papa and Grandmama have been crying a lot. I am sad too. Mostly because you're not here.

Love,

Clara

As Mrs. Bancroft said, Clara had signed her own name. At the sight of the childish handwriting, yet more tears flooded my eyes. I traced her signature with my finger. *Oh, Clara, it seems you and I need each other more than ever. If only I could be your mother.*

A feeling of guilt choked me. Was it wrong to love another woman's child when my own baby was with someone else, albeit someone who would love her as if she were her own? It was wrong—this pairing of the wrong woman with the wrong child, yet it was what women did. Our motherly instincts were not far below the surface, easily tugged from us when a child in need presented herself.

If only that had been true of my own mother. She'd been able to love Robbie with her whole heart. For Mauve and me, she saved only a small part of her capacity for affection to bestow upon us. Was it because he was a boy? Or her youngest?

But what if that were it? Mother could not love us after she lost a child. Her heart had been too shattered to love again. Did his death make her worry about losing us and if so, had she purposely shut down her feelings?

I thought of all the mornings after we lost Robbie that Mother stayed in her room, presumably in bed, if we were to believe the hushed mutterings of the servants. Had the sadness taken over her life? Pushed away any capacity for joy and love? If so, that was as sad as the fate of poor Mary Bancroft. They both suffered from ailments not apparent to the naked eye but debilitating just the same.

What part did my father have in Mother's retreat from the world? Had his coldness and cruelty contributed?

All these questions about my family were likely never to be answered. Was part of growing up accepting that we could not understand everything? Some things must be put aside in order to live the life we're yearning for. Otherwise, the endless loop of questions smothered a person.

None of it mattered anyway if they hanged me for a murder I didn't commit.

You're not alone, I reminded myself. The Bancrofts loved me. They wanted me to come home.

God, please make it so.

I SLEPT through the night on my hard little cot with only the thin blanket to keep me warm. When I woke to the dim light of morning, I yearned for a decent meal and a bath.

I didn't bother to get up, I simply rolled to my other side. Facing the wall, I stared at the indentations in the cold cement. Defeat and fear battled for dominance in my soul. I didn't want to die, but I also wouldn't make it long if life continued this way. A trapped and wounded animal. That's all I was now.

What would my sister think if she saw me now? Would she help if she could?

Those questions were shoved aside when the guard brought my breakfast. Despite the unappetizing look and smell of the pale, slimy porridge, I ate it all. Knowing that another meal wouldn't come soon and it would be small when it did, I could not be particular. After all, I was lucky to be fed.

I'd finished my meal and used the heinous bucket by the time the guard returned. He didn't flinch as he came inside to take both the tray and bucket. Still, I flushed at the sight. Could I endure more humiliation?

To my surprise, he returned about ten minutes later, carrying the dress I'd had on when they booked me.

"Good news, Miss Sullivan. You're being released."

I nearly fell off the cot in my haste to stand. "What? Did they agree to bail?"

"No, you're being cleared of all charges. Don't know why. But gather your things. I'm to walk you out to the lobby, where someone waits to take you home."

Sure enough, Mrs. Bancroft waited for me in the lobby. I expected her to joyfully embrace me, but instead, she gave me a somber look before squeezing my hand. "Come home. I'll explain everything there."

I nodded, feeling numb. This was not the reception I'd imagined. But I was free. I was going home.

Had Father confessed? No. He would never do so unless they'd questioned him and gotten him to confess somehow.

Mrs. Bancroft didn't say much as we headed home in the motorcar with Joseph at the wheel. By the time we arrived at the front door, I'd become almost lulled to sleep by the warmth of her body next to me. I'd been cold the entire time I was in my jail cell, and to be warm again felt like the best luxury in the world.

Soon, we were inside. Charlie came running into the foyer, wagging his tail so hard I worried it might fall off. I knelt to pull him into my arms, both of us giving kisses.

When Charlie had settled down, Mrs. Bancroft told me Penelope was waiting upstairs for me. "She has a bath prepared for you. Why don't you go up now and clean up while I speak with our cook about lunch. Percy's on his way home. He had an emergency with a patient this morning." She caressed my cheek. "You've been through too much for someone so young and innocent. Thank God you're home safe."

"I'm glad to be home with you. More so than I could ever say. Where's Clara?"

"She went out with her nanny. I wanted you to have a chance to bathe and dress before she leapt upon you. She's missed you terribly."

"I missed her."

"Go on now," Mrs. Bancroft said. "I'll see you in an hour or so."

Charlie and I hurried up the stairs to my room. Penelope greeted me tearfully. "Miss, I was frantic. I can't tell you how good it is to see your face."

"It's good to see yours too."

"How could they think you'd do something so awful?" Penelope asked. "They must be a bunch of idiots down there at the police station."

"I'm not sure what's happened, but I hope to have answers soon."

"For now, I have a hot bath ready for you. Leave your clothes in the hamper inside the bathroom, and I'll take care of washing them for you."

I happily sank into the hot, soapy water, grateful for the warmth that spread through my limbs and into my fingers and toes. Charlie, clearly afraid to be parted from me, refused to leave the bathroom, sitting next to the tub with his chin resting on his front legs. After a good soak, hair washing, and scrubbing, I stepped out to towel-dry and slip into my robe.

Penelope fixed my hair and helped me dress while she told me about Mrs. Landry and our kind neighbor Mr. Foster. "He's come by to take her for a walk every morning. I think they're smitten."

"How nice for her," I said. "She's been lonely since she lost her husband."

"Yes, but what will we do without her? If she marries, that is."

"We'll take it as it comes. What choice do we have, after all?"

"None at all, miss. After everything that's happened, we surely know that."

In no time at all, I was presentable and headed downstairs. I felt almost like my old self by the time I was seated at the dining room table and eating a bowl of the cook's delicious clam chowder and hunks of sourdough bread. Mrs. Bancroft ate with me, but Percival had not yet returned.

"Something bad's happened, hasn't it?" I finally asked after my stomach was full.

"When Percy arrives, we will sit down and talk through everything. Until then, let's retire to the sitting room. The cold seems to have crept into my bones."

While we waited, she filled me in on some of our patients. She'd had to call on them without me, and with everything on her mind, it had not been easy.

Finally, Percival arrived. He looked worse than the last time I'd seen him, with dark circles under his bloodshot eyes. I stood and gave him a tentative smile. "Hello, Percival."

He rushed to me and kissed my hand. "Thank God you're home. Thank you for waiting for me. I wanted to be here when we told you."

My stomach dropped. "Told me what?"

"Please, sit." Percy gestured toward the chair.

Once we were all seated and Percival had sent Robert downstairs, he turned to me. "I have bad news. Your mother's died."

My hands flew to my mouth. "What happened?"

"She took her own life," Percival said. "After confessing to killing Mary."

I couldn't understand what he meant—his words sounded almost like a foreign language. "Say that again." Charlie, sensing my distress, pressed against my leg.

"Your mother went to the asylum and led Mary outside. It was all laid out in her letter to the police. Which was delivered after her body was discovered by her maid."

"My mother killed her? But why?"

"She did it for you," Mrs. Bancroft said. "As misguided as it sounds, she wanted you and Percy to have a chance of a life together."

"But...but I don't understand. She wouldn't do that." I looked at each of them in turn, utterly bewildered.

"She sent you a letter as well," Mrs. Bancroft said, drawing an envelope from her pocket. "To this address." She handed it to me. "Would you like to read it alone?"

I stared at the envelope with my name written in Mother's perfect handwriting. "No, please stay." With trembling fingers, I unsealed the envelope and pulled out one of Mother's embossed pieces of stationery. My hands shook so badly that I could barely unfold it.

I had to force myself to look down at the final words my mother had written to me.

Dear Estelle,

By the time this reaches you, I will have done what I had to do. I have sent a letter to the police confessing to the murder of Mary Bancroft. I would like to tell you her murder was an accident, but that would be a lie. Here at the end of my life, I wish to tell you the truth.

I went to the asylum with the sole intent to lure her into the forest and leave her there. It may sound cold-blooded, and I suppose it was, but really, what kind of life was she living there? The situation was untenable for all. You and Percival are obviously in love. That you've chosen to do the honorable thing tells me a lot about the man he is as well as the woman you have grown into.

I have not been a good mother to you. Since we lost Robbie, I have not been able to engage in life as I should. Thus, you and your sister have been neglected in ways I'm deeply ashamed of.

You will ask yourself why. Therefore, I will say it clearly. I cannot live with the shame of my failures as a mother. I've lost you all. Living one more day with your father is not something I can face. In addition, I certainly do not want to go to prison. This is the only solution for all of us. Mary will be out of the way, carving out a path for your happiness with Percival and his family. You can be the mother to Clara that she needs. Mrs. Bancroft can be the mother you need.

This all will be a shock to you. I suppose you'll wonder how I could do such a thing. My only explanation is this: I am your mother, and I want your happiness more than my own. As they say, still waters run deep. That's always been true for me. The demons in my mind have outpaced my good intentions. For years, I've warred with myself to stay strong, but the overwhelming sadness only grows worse with time.

Be well, my dear daughter. I may not have said it enough, but I love you and I am proud of you. Please tell Mauve, should you ever see her again, how much I love her and how sorry I am. For everything.

Love,
Mother

TEARS FELL from my cheeks and landed on the paper, splashing the ink into puddles of regret and remorse. "She...she says she's sorry. For everything."

"Dear me, you poor thing." Mrs. Bancroft came to sit next to me on the sofa and pulled me into an embrace. "But she did the right thing. No good mother would let her daughter be convicted of a crime she didn't do. Especially one that could come with the death penalty."

"As you know, I went to see her yesterday," Percival said, appearing as stunned as I. "She gave me no reason to think she'd killed Mary. I think of myself as a man who can easily read people, especially given my line of work, but I had no idea it would come to this."

"I can't believe she did this," I whispered, pulling away from Mrs. Bancroft to gaze down at the letter I still held in quivering hands. "I'd not imagined she had it in her to protect me. Or to do something so drastic. For me, no less."

"Or maybe you didn't know her as well as you thought you did," Mrs. Bancroft said. "She's clearly struggled over the years."

"Married to a beast. Then losing Robbie. It was no wonder she couldn't get out of bed. But murder?" I shook my head, still utterly dumbfounded. "How can you not hate me? Either of you?"

"How could we hate you?" Mrs. Bancroft asked. "None of this is because of you."

"That's correct," Percival said sternly. "You're as innocent as we are."

"My family has caused yet more harm to yours," I said.

Percival shook his head, his expression grim. "Your family, but not you. We're all victims of this tragedy that began with a war between two criminals. And the truth is—Mary was very sick. I don't believe she was ever going to get better. As much as I hate this for Clara, I have to agree with your mother—what kind of life did Mary have there? All locked up. At the mercy of the staff." His eyes filled, and he swiped at them with the edge of his handkerchief. "My poor, troubled wife. What an end to a tragic life."

"I'm sorry," I whispered. Shame flooded me. Was God

punishing me for coveting another's husband? "I'd like to return to my apartment."

"Are you sure?" Percival asked.

"I need time to think," I said.

"Will you go home for your mother's funeral?" Mrs. Bancroft asked.

"I don't know. I don't know anything."

Mrs. Bancroft looked at me and then Percival, a determined set to her mouth, before rising to her feet. "I'm going up to see Clara. While I'm upstairs, I'll ask Penelope to pack your things."

I rose from the couch on shaking legs. "Thank you."

"I'll be over to check on you tomorrow." Mrs. Bancroft squeezed my shoulders. "All will be well. It may take some time, but we're all going to be fine."

After she left, I looked down at my hands, unsure what to do or say now that Percival and I were alone.

He came to stand beside me. "How tangled we are. Love is messy. Complicated."

"Never more so than between us. How can I look Clara in the eyes, knowing my mother took hers from her?"

"We've kept Clara protected for a reason. She'll not grieve a woman she never knew. Perhaps later, when she's an adult and can understand better what happened, she'll have questions. For now, she wants only for you to be part of her family." He brushed his knuckles against the apple of my cheek. "We must give it some time. All of us."

"Time for what?" I whispered.

"To grieve. To sort through all the complicated feelings we both have."

I nodded. "Yes. Time."

"Heals all wounds, right?" Percival asked.

"I certainly hope so."

"Please, let me know if you need anything."

I promised I would before leaving him to stand alone by the

fire. As I walked through the doorway, I glanced back. He'd already turned to face the hearth, his head bowed and his shoulders slumped.

PENELOPE and I returned to the apartment soon thereafter. She suggested I rest in my room until supper, and I didn't disagree. After helping me out of my dress and into my dressing gown, she tucked me into bed as if I were a child.

I had set the letter next to the bed and took it out to read it once again. Then I turned onto my side, curled up into a ball, and cried myself to sleep.

When I woke, no light was visible between the cracks in the drapes that covered the windows. I got up and drank a glass of water Penelope had left for me before sitting in the wingback chair with a blanket covering my legs. My loyal maid had lit a fire earlier, but it had died down, leaving only a few red embers. I placed several logs into the hearth and pulled back the curtains. The city's lights glowed and sparkled cheerfully but did nothing to lift the darkness inside my soul.

A few minutes later, Penelope arrived and asked if I'd rather have my supper on a tray than come downstairs. "Yes, that would be nice."

"Mrs. Landry's made your favorite—chicken potpie."

Normally, I would have been thrilled at the thought of the buttery crust and creamy filling, but I was too sad to care much about food. "Please thank her for me."

"Yes, I certainly will. I'll be back shortly," Penelope said. "Unless there's something I can get for you?"

I smiled up at her. "You're rather like a mother hen."

She flushed prettily. "I want only to comfort you but don't know how."

"Your mere presence is enough. Always."

Her eyes misted before she scurried out of the room, clearly embarrassed by her show of emotion.

She returned not long after, visibly shaking.

"What is it?" I sat up straighter, alarmed.

"Your father's here."

14

PERCIVAL

The afternoon was spent planning Mary's funeral. Simon had arrived not long after Stella left us, looking as if he hadn't slept in a week. He came in hot, demanding to know why Miss Sullivan, her name said with a sneer, had been let out of jail.

"You better sit for this," I said.

He looked at first as if he would argue with me, but instead he did as suggested.

"This is going to come as a shock to you. As it did myself and Miss Sullivan." I went on to explain the arrival of Stella's mother's letter admitting to the crime and her subsequent suicide.

"But why? Why would she harm Mary?"

I didn't answer right away, unsure how to say it without admitting to our feelings for each other. Of course, he'd guessed previously, but saying the words out loud made me feel guilty and ashamed.

"Do not answer," Simon said. "She wanted Miss Sullivan to have you to herself."

"Correct."

He cursed under his breath, shaking his head. "This family. They never cease in bringing us tragedy."

"Not Miss Sullivan. Her parents."

He glared at me with glittering eyes before getting up to pour himself a whiskey.

Ironic, I thought, given that his father and Mr. Sullivan killed over the illegal distribution of liquor. How much simpler it would have been if the Eighteenth Amendment had never been passed. Then again, Mr. Sullivan and my father-in-law had been involved in illegal business even before Prohibition.

"Did you hear me?" Simon asked, pulling me from my thoughts.

"No, sorry. What did you say?"

"I said we need to talk about Mary's funeral and burial."

We did so, working it out amicably despite our differences. She was to be laid to rest in the family plot with her father and mother. We agreed there would be no memorial service or wake. There was no one to mourn her but the two of us. When she'd entered the asylum over six years ago, she may as well have been dead already. No one from her previous circles cared to visit. Not after the rumors swept through town. Who knew if any of the gossip discussed the facts accurately. At the time, I'd been too brokenhearted to care.

"Have you been careful to lie low?" I asked Simon when the plan had been decided upon and handed off to Robert to arrange the details.

"I'd planned on taking the boat to England this morning," Simon said. "But as usual, the Sullivans have created more tragedy and trouble for us."

"Will you leave soon?"

"Yes, as soon as we have her in the ground, I'll get on a boat. I'm not sure I'll ever come back. I can't stand around and watch you marry the daughter of my enemy."

My first instinct was to deny that we would wed, but I

couldn't lie to Simon. Not after everything we'd been through together. "I'd like to be happy. It's not a crime."

"Enough of those have already been committed against my family." He threw back his whiskey in one swift flick of his wrist.

"I'm sorry for your pain. Truly. And for my own. And for Clara, who was growing up without a mother. But none of that is because of Miss Sullivan. She's been as hurt by Sean Sullivan as we have. Now her mother's dead too, after admitting to a heinous crime. I don't suppose you could summon any kindness for her?"

"Maybe someday. Right now, all I am is angry."

"And I cannot blame you."

He folded his hands under his chin as if in prayer, still peering at me but with less venom. "None of this is your fault either. Or mine. And, I grant you, Miss Sullivan's innocent as well. Why is it our lives have been ruined by the selfish acts of two men?"

"I don't know the answer. I know only that I want to be a good father to Clara—not like my own father who died in the arms of his mistress without a thought of me or my mother." My voice grew husky as I spoke about him. I rarely mentioned him or, for that matter, thought of him at all.

Simon left soon thereafter. A few minutes later, the nanny brought Clara in to see me. My daughter climbed onto my lap and snuggled against my chest.

I hadn't yet told her the good news about Stella, and as I breathed in the sweet smell of her head, I had no idea how to explain. Yes, Stella was out of jail, but her mother had confessed to the murder before ending her own life. It all sounded so sordid and sad. How could a six-year-old understand any of it? I barely did myself.

"Stella has been released from jail," I said. "They've caught the person who...harmed your mother." I hated to say the word *murder* in front of a child. Was there any hope my sweet little girl would come through her childhood intact? Her young life had been one blow after another since the day she was born.

"Will she come home to us, then?" Clara asked.

"She's gone home to her own apartment."

"Can I visit her?"

"Not today but perhaps another time," I said. "Your grandmother gave her your letter, and she was pleased to receive it—I think it cheered her immensely."

"Good." She nestled more deeply into my chest. What did she think of in that little head of hers? "Papa, are you sad?"

"I am. Are you?"

"Only because you are," she said.

"I won't be sad forever."

"Then I shan't be either."

Hoping to distract her from unhappy subjects, I asked her questions about her day. How had school been, and was she happy to see her friends now that school had begun for the new year? She chattered on in her chirpy, adorable voice. As low as I was, my daughter never ceased to warm my heart.

15

STELLA

Penelope helped me dress quickly and fixed my hair while my father apparently waited for us in the sitting room. I was shaking by the time I went out to greet him. He stood with his hands behind his back near the bay window that looked out at the street and beyond the park. I watched him for a moment, mesmerized by the slight sway of his body as if he were listening to music.

"Father?"

He turned to face me, his face drawn and pinched. Was it possible Mother's death had been a blow to him?

"Estelle, good evening."

"Would you like to sit?"

"Yes, that would be nice, thank you."

We sat across from each other, the coffee table between us. I set aside the needlepoint I'd started last week. How long ago that seemed now.

"May I offer refreshment?" I asked.

He shook his head. "I won't be here long."

"Why *are* you here?"

"I wanted to tell you in person that your mother's funeral

will be held the day after tomorrow. She asked to be buried in the plot on our property. Next to Robbie."

"Did she leave you a letter too?"

"Yes. She mentioned she sent one to you and the police. Her confession seems to have done what it needed to do."

"I'm free if that's what you mean."

He appeared to gather his thoughts before speaking. "Your mother was only eighteen years old when we married. At the time our ten-year age difference didn't seem relevant, but looking back upon it, I can see clearly how young she was."

"What's that to do with anything?"

"Nothing other than to say we didn't really know each other well when we married."

"Were you surprised by what she did?" I asked. "Did you have any inkling about what she'd done to Mary?"

"Not a one."

"She said she did it for me, which baffles me."

"Isn't that what mothers do? Isn't that what you did?"

My breath caught. He was right. I had sacrificed for Mireille as naturally and instinctively as if it had resided inside me from the moment I was born.

"I suppose I came here to say this to you—if you're wondering why she did it and if she had any regrets, then don't."

"How do you know what she thought at the end? Before she...took her life." I couldn't bring myself to say how she did it. The images in my imagination were enough to bring me to my knees.

"Mothers—most anyway—will do whatever it takes for their child to be happy. Therefore, she died without regrets."

"But she murdered an innocent woman."

"Are we certain she's telling the truth about that?" Father asked.

I gaped at him and jarred into silence. "You think she lied? Just to help me?"

"When she discovered they'd arrested you, it set everything into motion. I don't think your mother was capable of murder. She is capable, however, of saving you from a wrongful conviction."

Oh, Mother, what did you do?

"If she didn't murder Mary Bancroft, then who did?" I asked.

"That I don't know. I know only that it was not I, as hard as that may be for you to believe. I've no interest in harming a poor woman like that—as sick as she was. It's not as if she could damage me or my reputation."

I took my hankie from my sleeve, twisting it around my fingers, thinking through what he'd said. Was it possible it had been an accident? Had Mary wandered outside without the staff seeing her?

"There's something else I must say before I go," Father said. "They jailed you to get to me. For that, I'm sorry."

"Do you think so, really?"

"The cops and I have been dancing for a while. They'd love to catch me, but so far they haven't been able to. I'd really like to keep it that way."

"Mother gave you a convenient way out, didn't she?"

"I doubt that was foremost in her mind, but regardless, they no longer suspect me."

"Did you tell Mother they had me jailed to get to you?" I asked.

"I'm afraid I did not have that opportunity."

"She might not have done what she did had she known." Fury rose within me without warning, nearly making me sick. I pressed my hankie against my mouth.

"We cannot change the past, my dear." He rose to his feet. "The funeral will be at two in the afternoon the day after tomorrow. I do hope to see you there."

With that, he turned and headed toward the foyer and was

out the door before I could say anything further. Just as well. I had nothing to say to the man. Not today. Maybe never again.

———

THE NEXT MORNING, I walked to Percival's apartment with the sole purpose of telling the Bancrofts about the visit from my father. The moment I stepped out to the street, bitter wind nipped at my cheeks. More snow had come during the night, but by morning the cloud cover had departed, which made temperatures drop drastically. Thus, the roads were icy and treacherous. Although I wore a scarf, a hat, and my wool coat, and my hands were stuffed inside a muff, the cold crept into my bones.

Regardless of my low mood and icy weather, the city felt alive with the hustle and bustle of a weekday in the city. I joined the fashionable crowd, making their way down the avenue. Men in tailored suits and fedoras walked with purpose, their breath visible in the cold air. Women glided by in fur stoles, their hats pulled low against the chill. Children, bundled up in woolen coats and knickers, laughed and played in the snow and skated on patches of ice, their joy infectious enough to bring a smile to my face despite my troubles.

The scent of roasted chestnuts wafted from a vendor's cart as I passed by. Cars and horse-drawn carriages shared the street with clanging streetcars, the cacophony of city life blending with the occasional jazz tune from a nearby street performer. Icicles hung from awnings, sparkling in the bright morning sunshine.

I loved this city, I realized. Somehow, even though I'd had troubles and frightening times since coming here, New York had crept into my soul and planted itself for good. Having been locked away, albeit for a short time, I had a renewed appreciation for the vibrant life that surrounded me in every direction. How good it was to be free.

As I approached Percival's building, I quickened my pace, a desire to see him like a physical pain. I used the knocker at the front door and waited, stomping my feet for warmth. Seconds later, Robert showed me in.

"Miss Stella, how are you managing?" Robert asked kindly.

"I'm not in jail." I smiled. "Thank you for asking."

"Thanks be to God."

"It gives one a new perspective, that is certain," I said.

"I, for one, am glad you're free and safe."

"You're kind to say so."

"I'll let Dr. Bancroft know you've arrived."

I thanked him again and while I waited, paced in front of the window.

"Stella?"

At the sound of my name coming from Percival's mouth, I turned around to see him standing there. The sight of him made me want to weep. I apologized for arriving without warning, which he brushed aside.

"How are you?" Percival asked. "Did you sleep?"

"Not much. You?"

"I slept better than expected. There comes a point when a body has to sleep despite all our worries." He stepped closer, his eyes warm and sympathetic. "Has something happened? What brings you by?"

"My father visited me yesterday. They're burying my mother tomorrow, and he asked that I be there."

"Do you want to go?"

"I'm unsure. However, there's more." I told him more about the conversation I'd had with my father. "All of which now has me wondering if my mother was truly guilty. She may have done this to save me." I paused, fighting tears. "Maybe she didn't want to live anymore, and taking the blame for Mary's death was her last act before she gave in to the darkness. But I really can't say. My head's jumbled and confused."

"It's to be expected." He took one of my hands and held it to his chest. "You and I need only to get through these next days and weeks. To reconcile everything that's happened so that we might emerge into a new life."

"Together?" I asked in a whisper.

"As terrible as it is to admit to this, I want nothing more than to be with you."

"But we mustn't act on our feelings. Not yet."

"It wouldn't be right. We're both too vulnerable. If we are to have hope for a future, we must continue down the moral path. Otherwise, guilt will ruin any possibility of a union between us. Do you understand?"

"I do. We must not feel as if we're committing a sin simply because we're selfish."

"As hard as it is, I think time apart will serve us well. Go and help to bury your mother. I'll do the same for Mary. Then, when we are done and our hands are still clean, we'll come back to each other."

"It's always been you and me since the first day, hasn't it?" I asked.

"It has."

Percival walked me to the door and gently kissed my hand. "I'll be thinking of you until we meet again."

"Take the time you need."

But not forever.

IN THE END, I decided to attend Mother's burial and memorial. I took the train up early the next morning, arriving at the church just as the service began. I didn't want to, but I sat in the front pew next to my father. I couldn't help but think that when we once were five, we were now only two.

As the service began, my thoughts drifted to my sister. I had not yet written to her, even though Pierre had given me the address before he left. It had been easier for me not to write. If I'd written to her with the truth of my new circumstances, she would have wanted to do something to help me. And I knew, deep down, that it was better for Mireille if I cut all ties.

But now? I had to tell her Mother had died. Although there was nothing she could do, it was her right to know what had happened.

After the preacher had finished the service, Father and I, in addition to most of our staff, went out to the burial plot and watched them lower her coffin into the cold ground. I took a rose from the bouquet someone had brought and knelt to toss it into the grave. "I'm sorry, Mother. For all your pain and loneliness. I hope you're finally at peace."

I put a different rose on the small grave of my little brother. They were together now. At least that gave me some comfort.

We all returned to the house, where the staff had prepared sandwiches and miniature cakes for the mourners. I did my best to play the part of a loving daughter, thanking people for coming and listening politely as they told me a story or two about Mother. Finally, everyone was gone, and I sighed a breath of relief. I found my father in his den, pouring himself a drink.

"Will you stay tonight?" Father asked.

As much as I'd like to have said no, I didn't have it in me to travel all the way back to the city at this late hour. "I'll stay in my old room if that's all right?"

He nodded, sinking into his favorite leather chair by the fire. "Your mother's maid will help you prepare for bed."

"Thank you." Mother's maid, Molly, had greeted me earlier, her eyes puffy from crying. I'd felt sorry for her. Who knew what would happen to her now? There were no women to care for in this house.

"Would you like a drink? Your mother often had a sherry this time of evening." He said it as if I hadn't lived here for most of my life.

"No, thank you. I'll retire shortly. It's been a long day."

"She would have approved of the service and the way the staff handled the wake, don't you think?" Father asked.

"I do, yes."

We were interrupted by James informing us that the police were here. "I've shown them into the library, sir."

Father and I exchanged a quick glance. Why were they here?

"May I join you?" I asked.

"If you must." Father got up, a soft groan escaping his lips.

It was Chief Wallace who waited, warming his hands by the fire. He stood to greet us, but Father told him to remain sitting as he and I sat together on the sofa.

"I've come with news of the case," Wallace said. "Call it an old cop's instinct, but I didn't believe it was Mrs. Sullivan who did this despite her confession. Thus, I returned to the asylum and poked around, asking questions of the staff. Finally, I found an orderly willing to speak to me. The vow of silent loyalty among staff members is a serious thing but not completely unbreakable. They look out for one another and cover mistakes if they have to, but I managed to get the truth out of him. He said one of the other orderlies left the door unlocked. Not on purpose, mind you, but because he was new to the job and simply forgot. He didn't want to tell the truth for fear of trouble for himself and his friends. However, he saw Mary Bancroft walk outside of her own volition. At the time, he thought a nurse was going with her."

"They didn't think to tell you this before they arrested my daughter?" Father asked angrily. "Or before my wife took her life?"

"As I said, he was afraid. These men work for paltry wages, yet they're happy for the work and don't want to lose it. The young man in question told me Mary Bancroft asked to go outside almost every evening. If there was a nurse available during warm weather, sometimes they would take her out and walk with her on the grounds. When I asked Mrs. Mason if this was true, she confirmed that Mary had an obsession with being outside whenever they would allow her to do so. She also said they indulged her if the weather were decent, mostly because it helped Mary to sleep better. With exercise, she had fewer outbursts in the middle of the night and that kind of thing."

"Then who was the strange woman who came to visit her?" I asked.

"She didn't exist," Wallace said. "The orderly made her up as a distraction."

"Who else knew about the unlocked door?" I asked.

"According to the orderly, no one but himself and a few of the others. The young man who left the door open didn't show up for work this morning, which is why the orderly was willing to tell the truth. From what he said, everyone was intimidated by him. He's large and violent, apparently. This was told to me by several of the staff."

"And this orderly's gone?" Father asked. "The one who left the door open?"

"We can only assume he's fled." Wallace scratched behind his ear, cocking his head to the left. "This has been a strange case, I must say. My colleagues in New York City were convinced it was you, Miss Sullivan, but I didn't think so."

"It was an accident," I said, speaking more to myself than the others.

A voice whispered to me. *She did it for you.*

She loved me, after all.

Poor Mother. She must have felt alone.

"I came to tell you what I learned but also to apologize for my colleagues in the city. If it led to your mother taking her own life, then I'm truly sorry."

"My wife's suffered from hysteria and unexplained sadness for decades," Father said without emotion. "Doing something for Estelle gave her peace. She left the earth knowing she'd saved at least one of her children."

"Her sadness wasn't *unexplained*," I spoke more forcefully than I thought I had in me. "She wasn't the same after we lost Robbie. He died when he was only two," I said to Wallace. "Mother never fully recovered."

"The loss of a child is not something one recovers from," Wallace said quietly. "The wife and I lost one of our precious daughters when she was only four. My dear wife's found a way to go on, mostly because our other children need her. Regardless, for both of us, it's a hole in our heart that will remain until we meet her again in heaven."

"That will be lovely," I said, smiling at the thought of seeing Robbie again.

"I imagine this has been a trying day," Wallace said. "I'll take my leave."

We all stood. Father shook the detective's hand before walking him into the foyer. I stayed behind, gathering myself. When I'd been here the other day to see Mother, I thought it would be the last time. After tomorrow morning, I'd have no reason to return. Father and I would not have a relationship if we'd ever had one at all. Although I'd never be able to prove it, he had killed Connie. For that, I could not forgive him.

Later, before I slept in my childhood bedroom for the last time, I sat down at the desk to write my sister a letter. It would take me more than a page or two to tell her everything that had transpired since I saw her last. I was sorry to have to share with her the tragedy that had become our family, but she must know that our mother was gone.

16

PERCIVAL

Laying my wife to rest was as hard as I thought it would be. Simon wept through the entire graveside service. Mother stood by my side, lending much-needed support, but she, too, cried. We'd left Clara with her nanny, as I saw no reason to put her through all of it.

Sadly, it was the three of us, in addition to Mrs. Mason and a few of the nurses, who had cared for Mary over the years and no one else. When we'd married, the church had been full. Mary and I in love, and bursting with hope. Who knew everything could go so horribly wrong?

We returned home to a light supper that tasted of sand. Simon was set to leave on a ship sailing to the south of France in the morning. He'd said he would not likely return to live but that he would be back for visits. "I mustn't let Clara grow up without knowing any of her mother's family."

"You're welcome here anytime," I said. "But you must understand, my life will go on. I plan on marrying Miss Sullivan."

"Although it makes me sick to my stomach to hear, what you do with the rest of your life is not my concern. And truthfully,

169

you've been loyal to my sister when most wouldn't have been. I have no hard feelings for you, only love."

"And I for you."

At the first morning light, I bade him farewell, wishing him the best and asking if he'd please write every so often.

When the car pulled away from the curb, I stood in the frigid dawn and watched them merge into the busy traffic until they were no longer visible. Then I went inside and sat by the fire, drinking a cup of coffee and thinking about what was to come.

It was only right that I should wait to ask Stella to marry me. There should be a period of mourning even if it had actually started six years ago when I'd had to have her committed to the asylum. I wished I could marry her tomorrow and begin a life with her as my wife and Clara's stepmother, but all would come in good time.

I would court her, take her to dinner and for walks in Central Park, and all the other things one would do with the woman one intended to marry. She deserved to have a proper courtship.

I had breakfast with Mother, both of us quiet. We were just finishing up when Robert announced the arrival of Detective Forsyth. "Show him into the sitting room," I said, heart sinking. Would this ever end?

Robert nodded. A few minutes later, I joined the detective.

"I'm sorry to come at such an early hour," Forsyth said. "I have something to tell you that couldn't wait."

"Yes, of course. What can I do for you?"

"I've heard from Chief Wallace up north. Your wife's death has been ruled an accident." He went on to tell me that an orderly had admitted that his colleague left the door open and that he himself had seen her walk outside. The supposed woman who visited was a ruse to deflect the guilt of the young men in question. "There will be no more inquiries made."

"Has Miss Sullivan been informed?" I asked.

"Yes, Wallace went to the house and told both her and her father what we'd learned."

After he was gone, I found Mother and relayed all of it to her. She said nothing at first, simply shaking her head, clearly sorry for Mrs. Sullivan. Mother's kind heart could not stand to think of the suffering all of this had caused, including two innocent women. One of whom I loved.

"And Stella knows?"

I nodded. "She does."

Mother sank into a chair, her cheeks stripped of color. "She sacrificed for her daughter. One last act of motherhood."

I rubbed my eyes. "It's all so tragic."

"Do you think Mary wandered out because she wanted to… die?"

Somehow, that had not occurred to me. "It's possible."

"She hated being confined. Perhaps she'd had enough."

"I don't know if that makes me feel better or worse."

We sat in silence for a few minutes. Everything had changed and then changed again in the course of only days. It was mind-boggling how different everything was now compared to just last week at this time.

"You should go see Stella today," Mother said. "She'll have returned from her father's and will need support."

"We agreed to stay away from each other for a period of time. Probably weeks."

"Why?" Mother stared at me with one of her penetrating gazes.

"Propriety. Because it's like dancing on Mary's grave."

"Nonsense. You and Stella have conducted yourselves with honor. There's no reason to punish yourselves further. Go to her. Have supper with her. Talk to her."

"Yes, fine. If you think it's the right thing to do, then I shall."

"You've known my thoughts on the matter."

"Mother, you're incorrigible."

"So they say." She sniffed and picked up her needlework. "I've no one to see today and plan to spend a cozy day inside. I'm exhausted."

"You've been wonderful, Mother. Through everything, I've been able to count on you. I don't know the last time I thanked you."

"Not necessary. You're my precious son. I would do anything for you. Most mothers will, you know."

"If you and Stella are the example, then I must agree."

My heart felt lighter than it had in years, and yet the weight of tragedy still lived inside me. It was possible that both things could be true—I could mourn Mary's tragic life and love Stella at the same time.

Either way, the events unfolded as they had, and I owed it to myself, Mother, and Clara to begin a new chapter. One in which I hoped we would all be happy. God willing.

17

STELLA

A spring morning, with cherry trees in full bloom, matching the color of my precious daughter's baby cheeks, I sat in a rocker by the window. Emmeline had just turned six months old the day before. She'd been an easy baby thus far and grew more so with every passing day. Although I'd loved her madly from the beginning, the last few months her personality had begun to show. Quick to giggle and babble, I felt certain she would be good-natured and talkative. Her brown curls and fair skin were very much like my own, but her eyes and mouth were all Percival.

I lifted her to my shoulder and patted her back, coaxing a burp from her tiny body. Satiated, she snuggled into my shoulder and fell asleep. Just as I rose up and placed her in the cradle, I heard the footsteps of Percival and Clara coming down the hallway. I'd left the nursery door open, and they stepped inside, careful not wake Emmeline.

They came to stand next to me, each taking one of my hands, followed by Charlie, who rarely left Clara's side these days. The three of us gazed down with adoration at the tiny sleeping form for a moment before heading out of the room. Percival let go of my hand to close the nursery softly behind us.

I smiled down at Clara. She looked smart in a sailor-style dress. Her hair had been tied back with yellow ribbons. We smiled at each other, mother and daughter now. The chosen kind.

"Hello, darling." Percival leaned close to kiss my cheek. "You're looking lovely this afternoon."

I flushed with pleasure. Having been denied our intimate times for six weeks after I gave birth to Emmeline, we had been making up for it in the weeks that followed. So much so that I suspected I might already be pregnant again. I'd not confirmed it, so I hadn't said anything to my husband. There would be plenty of time for that.

"Where have you two been?" I asked.

"We've been shopping," Clara said. "Finding something for your birthday, Mama."

Mama. Clara was the first child to call me Mama, and it had changed my life. Hearing the word come out of her mouth the day after our wedding had nearly brought me to my knees. Although my biological baby remained far away in the arms of my dear sister, I had Clara to love and nurture. She was my daughter as much as Emmeline or any of the children who might come later. We'd been lost—Clara needing a mother and me craving a child to love with my whole heart—until we found each other.

"But my birthday isn't for another week," I said as we made our way down the stairs for tea.

"Yes, but Papa said we couldn't wait for the last minute. We have to find the exact perfect gift."

"Which we did." Percival winked at me over Clara's head.

"I have everything I need or want already," I said, smiling back at him.

Mrs. Bancroft waited for us in the sitting room. She had

come back from her morning rounds only to be called out again. I worried she worked too much, especially now that I was so busy with the children. However, she didn't seem inclined to slow down anytime soon.

Penelope, who had come home with me once Percival and I married, arrived with a tray of sandwiches and our tea. She'd been such a help to me as I adjusted to my new life as a wife and mother. Mrs. Landry had married our neighbor Mr. Foster shortly after Percival and I wed. She and Mr. Foster were now happily living in his apartment with a baby of their own coming soon. Mr. Foster had acquired a teaching position at a public school in Manhattan thus their financial circumstances were better than they had been. In more wonderful news, he had a New York editor interested in his novel. We were all on pins and needles waiting to hear if it was to be published.

Our former nanny had retired, and we'd hired a new girl, fresh from England, whom we all adored. Between Mrs. Bancroft, Clara, Percival, and me, the nanny had an easy job. We'd all fallen so completely in love with Emmeline I worried she'd be spoiled rotten—all the more reason to have more children.

We chatted about our days, with Clara entertaining us with stories from school. She'd recently discovered her nemesis in the form of a boy named Leo. Almost every afternoon, she had a tale to share about his endless teasing. One day after school, the headmistress had taken me aside to inform me that Clara had punched Leo in the nose. When I asked what provoked such a response, the headmistress had given me a mischievous smile. "He called her a weak little girl. She didn't take kindly to his depiction of her."

"Yes, but she mustn't resort to violence," I'd said, stifling my own amusement. God bless this poor Leo. He had no idea who he was coming up against if he thought our Clara weak.

"You may punish her as you see fit," the headmistress had

said. "As for me, although it hurts me to do so, I've informed her that she must stay after school for a week to help me to clean classrooms."

I had yet to hear from Mauve. Whether it was that the address was wrong or that she couldn't find it in herself to write back, I did not know. Each night before I fell asleep, I prayed they were safe and well, wherever they were. I'd not given up hope of someday being reunited with them, but for now, I must focus on my family.

My father had recently sold his estate and disappeared. No one knew where or how. As time passed, I thought of him less and less. However, every few months, I visited my mother and Robbie in the graveyard, bringing flowers and cleaning their headstones.

After our tea, Percival and I went upstairs to rest some before it was time to change for supper. The baby woke still for feeding in the middle of the night, and I found naps helped to keep me from succumbing to sleep deprivation.

I lay on our bed and curled up on my side. Percival did the same, facing me and stroking my cheek.

"How are you feeling?" Percival asked.

"What do you mean?"

"You're pregnant again, aren't you?"

My eyes flew open in surprise. "How did you know?"

"I'm a doctor."

I laughed. "But not my doctor."

"Yes, but my powers of observation are keen. It's not been so long since you were expecting Emmeline that I can't recall the particular shade of green that accompanies the first trimester."

I swatted his shoulder. "You shouldn't tell a pregnant woman she looks green."

"You're not green now." He smiled cheekily. "In fact, you're blooming, which tells me you've just passed into the second trimester."

"I thought I couldn't get pregnant while nursing."

"Not always the case, which happily is not so now," Percival said.

"Are you pleased?"

"More than I can say." He kissed me softly. "You've made every dream of mine come true."

"And you mine."

"We made it through to the other side. After all the tragedy, here we are, with our growing family and each other. I'm a blessed man."

"You certainly are," I said, teasing. "And so am I."

He shifted onto his back and patted his chest. "Come rest here, my lovely wife. You deserve a nap."

I did as suggested, snuggling close with my head on his chest and my arm over his stomach. It was safe here in his arms. The love and home I'd wanted so badly was in the beating of his heart.

"You're all I could ever want," I whispered sleepily.

"Good. I don't plan to go anywhere else but here with you and our girls."

Content, I yawned and closed my eyes. Just then, inside my womb, a flutter-like butterfly wings reminded me of the child who would soon bless us further. In my darkest moments of despair, had I known this awaited me, I would have had more faith that hard times did not remain forever. Each day brought the promise of redemption.

In the six months after his wife's death, Percival courted me properly as if all that we'd endured together previously had been wiped clean. Of course, the past had not been swept away, as this is not the way of the world. The past hurts, and betrayals remained in our hearts, but we did not allow them to keep us from the life we deserved.

I'd thought many times in those first months of our blissful marriage that the difficulties we faced had made us stronger and more compassionate. Would we rather not have gone through them? Yes. However, without the hardships and darkness, perhaps we would be unable to recognize our blessings and when they'd finally arrived.

As I drifted off to sleep, I told myself to remember during times of trial that one must hold on, knowing joy would come back around if we remained faithful to what was right and good, even when it felt like more than we could bear.

Someday, I would tell my girls this lesson should they falter.

Stay strong during times of adversity. Be thankful in times of abundance. Love with all your heart.

MORE BOOKS BY TESS

EMERSON PASS HISTORICALS

The School Mistress

The Spinster

The Scholar

The Problem Child

The Seven Days of Christmas

The Musician

The Wordsmith

The Rebel

EMERSON PASS CONTEMPORARIES

The Sugar Queen

The Patron

The Pet Doctor

The Correspondent

The Innkeeper

Haven Moon

BLUE MOUNTAIN
Blue Midnight

Blue Moon

Blue Ink

Blue String

Blue Twilight

RIVER VALLEY
Riversong

Riverbend

Riverstar

Riversnow

Riverstorm

Tommy's Wish

LEGLEY BAY
Caramel and Magnolias

Tea and Primroses

CASTAWAY CHRISTMAS
Come Tomorrow

Promise of Tomorrow

SOUL SISTERS
Christmas Rings

Christmas Star

STANDALONES
Duet For Three Hands

Miller's Secret

The Santa Trial

ABOUT TESS

Hello!

I'm so happy you've found me! Here's a little about me.

I'm a proud mother. A loving wife. A woman of faith. A daughter to aging parents. A best friend.

I write fiction about people like you and me. Characters who deserve second chances and love and redemption and have had heartbreak and joy and everything in between.

I worry about my aging parents and my kids and sometimes wonder if I'm doing a good job as a mother or a daughter.

I have two cats I adore and take too many photos of. Mittens is a tuxedo and sleeps on my desk. Midnight hardly leaves Cliff's side, but I don't hold it against her even though she was my cat first.

I hate cooking dinner. My cakes always fall apart, even when I use a mix. I'm a little messy, especially when I have a deadline. I'm forgetful, which I blame on the stories in my head that distract me from real life. I'm always trying to lose ten pounds. I love Zumba and strength training classes at my local YMCA even though my knees sometimes ache. I love nothing better than to read all day in bed. As I grow older, I find myself liking books about good people and happy endings than works of great literary merit that leave me feeling sad. Sorry, but that's just the truth. If it were between French fries or a cookie, I would always go for the potatoes. I love sappy, sentimental movies and binge-watching series, especially Masterpiece

Theatre, country music, wine, flowers, birds, the beach and snuggling on the couch.

I work hard because I love what I do and never want to squander the opportunities God has given me. There's never a day I'm not thankful to my readers. Without them, I would not have my dream life, sitting at my desk and writing from my heart. I'm also blessed with a team behind the scenes who do *all the things* so I can write.

My best friend is Violet. She's brilliant and kind and a second mother to my girls. She makes me laugh and warms my heart even during the hardest times. I can tell her everything and never feel judged. She's just the best. You know what I mean because you probably have a Violet too.

My daughters, Emerson and Ella, are the pride of my life. They're both smart, compassionate, hard workers, and the most amazing humans. Honestly, I thank God every day for giving me the chance to be their mom. Although they're now young ladies, I still see the babies and little girls they once were. They'll always be my babies no matter how old they are. Sniff.

My stepsons, who I refer to as my Bonus Sons, are now adults forging their own way in the world and making us proud with their independence. I didn't have long with them, so I can't really take much credit, but I love them and am humbled and honored to be part of their lives.

And then there's Cliff. My soulmate. My partner in life. Cliff and I found each other when we were in our middle forties, after years of heartache for both of us. I was divorced with two little girls, and he was a widower raising two teenage boys on his own. We met through an online dating app! Tinder, of all places. I know, the odds of us finding each other were astronomical, especially on a dating app designed for young people. Honestly, it was nothing short of a miracle! We committed to going through the rest of our lives as a team and I can tell you without a doubt he was the best decision of my life. Cliff has supported my writing dreams, even during the years of struggle and disappointments. He always believed in my talent even when I wasn't so sure. All the success I have now is because of him. He's my WHY for all things. Recently, we moved into our dream house on a small lake. I'm still pinching myself.

That's a bit about me. I'd love to hear from you. Send me your bullet list so I can get to know a few things about you. Until then, I send love to you and yours.

Made in United States
Orlando, FL
08 December 2024

55195282R10104